Against All Obstacles

Jennifer Safrey

Against All Obstacles
Copyright © 2023 Jennifer Safrey
All rights reserved.

ISBN: (ebook) 978-1-958136-69-0
(print) 978-1-958136-77-5

Inkspell Publishing
207 Moonglow Circle #101
Murrells Inlet, SC 29576

Edited By Audrey Bobek
Cover Art By Fantasia Frog

DEDICATION

For Teddy

JENNIFER SAFREY

CHAPTER 1

His opening line, "Is this seat taken?" was unoriginal, but when it came to opening lines, Rachel didn't trust clever. She was a get-it-done type of woman. She preferred a man to be direct.

She had been nursing a bottle of water, the only kind of liquid she'd be drinking for the next three days. Being alone in her room made her antsy and restless, so she sat at the hotel bar instead. This weekend, this hotel was full of people with similar interests to hers, maybe similar experiences. She was open to a little amiable conversation.

But *this* guy... His body said, *Forget the conversation.* His mouth said, "Is this seat taken?" He had a charming English accent, no less. Rachel nodded at the seat and decided to see what came next. That was what this weekend was supposed to be all about, after all. Seeing what was next, and next, and next. And getting through it all.

He slid into the seat beside her. The smooth motion suggested he was an athlete. She trailed a finger up her plastic water bottle, and her skin came away wet with condensation.

He smiled at her and asked the bartender for a bottled water, which was no surprise to Rachel. He then turned to her and put out his hand. "Evan."

She took his hand. It completely engulfed hers. "Rachel."

Evan raised a brow as he released their grip, and Rachel knew why. "Quite a handshake. I confess I didn't expect that."

"That's what everyone says," she said. "When I was in college, I met a professor who cracked all my knuckles when she shook my hand. I promised myself I'd forever shake hands the same way. Men never expect it."

"Oh, I didn't mean—" Evan began.

"No, I'm sure you didn't. It's okay. I don't think a lot of women give a good grip. So men, out of politeness, I suppose, loosen their own grip. By the time they realize my handshake is the dominant one, it's too late for them to compensate." She grinned.

Evan grinned back. "Amazing. Well, if your first impression of absolutely beautiful woman hadn't done it for me, that handshake certainly would have. Well done."

Though she appreciated the compliment, there couldn't be much behind it. She happened to know this particular weekend, this particular New Hampshire hotel—and therefore, this particular hotel bar—was filled with mostly men. There were a lot more men to compare him to than there were women for him to compare her to. In her charcoal-gray leggings; long, soft hooded pink sweatshirt; and elastic headband, perhaps she provided an interesting view.

Now, the view *he* provided...

Evan had stepped straight from the pages of an outdoorsy catalog, the kind most people merely paged through while coveting the lifestyle. His blond hair was an artful muss on his head, long enough to run exploring fingers through but not so long it suggested barbershop neglect. His eyes were the blue of a summer-morning sky the first day after seven days and nights of gray downpour. He wore a short-sleeved purple nylon rash guard that hugged an extraordinarily athletic torso. Most of the men in this hotel this weekend were similarly built, but Evan was somehow even a cut above. Rachel fought the urge to giggle at how hilariously hot he was. And at how, as luck would have it, she was in zero position to take advantage of the few moments he'd bother with her.

The bartender slid the damp water bottle to Evan, and like she had, he waved away the offer of a glass. He downed half of it in one gulp, then had the grace to flash an embarrassed smile at her. "Sorry," he said. "I didn't mean to be rude. But I've been daydreaming about a bottle of water for at least an hour."

"You look like you've been working out," Rachel said.

"Yes. Well, not really. Just warming up," he said. "You may have noticed a lot of guys are in town for this race."

A lot of guys in town, indeed. "Race?" she asked, lifting a brow.

"The Golden Crucible," he clarified. "It's this crazy event—you don't want to know." He shook his head. "What brings you here? Some mountain hiking? Outlet shopping?"

"Wait, back up," Rachel said. "The Golden Crucible? Sounds, um, medieval."

He grinned. "That could be the most accurate word for it. It's rumored to be a sort of medieval torture."

"Torture? How long is the race? Longer than a ... marathon?"

"Ultimately. It's a forty-eight-hour race."

"What?" Rachel was worried she didn't inject enough incredulity into that word, but he didn't call her out.

"Yeah, we start Friday night—tomorrow night—and finish Sunday night. The competitors don't know what the race entails. It's an obstacle-course race, and nothing has been revealed ahead of time. We don't know the total distance. We don't know what we will be asked to do."

"You mean, like climbing, jumping, stuff like that?"

He took another pull of water and nodded. "Climbing,

jumping, digging, carrying heavy stuff, or dragging heavy stuff. I have no idea. I did some research on past The Golden Crucibles but it's not worth finding out because they try to make every race different."

"So, you don't have any idea what's going to happen for—hours, days?"

"I know a few things. It will be hot during the day but cold at night. No matter how much I trained, there will be things I've never done before. Most people who start can't finish, or give up before they finish."

"Then ... why?" she asked. "Why bother? It doesn't sound safe."

"It's a lot of things, but safe isn't one of them, no."

"I suppose" — Rachel lowered her voice conspiratorially — "the prize money is an incentive?"

"Nah. I mean, maybe, but ... that's not what motivates me. It's not that much."

Seventy-five hundred dollars isn't that much? Rachel wanted to ask. But she didn't. Because this was way too much fun.

"What motivates you, then?"

"The experience," he said. "It's been a while since ... since I had any kind of accomplishment like this. I've been out of sports for a while. But I don't want to—what do you do, Rachel? For work?"

Interesting. She'd thought he'd be much more braggy, display much more machismo. Except for one major judgment blunder, he was pretty straightforward and—nice. "I'm a high school math and science teacher."

"Wow," he said. She liked how it came out. Not wow as in *wow, boring*, but wow as in *wow, interesting*. "You must love your job. Getting kids excited about the way the world works."

"That's right," she said, "and I never thought of it in quite that phrasing before. 'The way the world works.' The big picture. Yes. They want to make such a difference, all of them, even the ones who pretend they don't care. They all want to be important, create things, figure things out. So I foster an environment for them to start to do big things."

"Do you see any future doctors, engineers, astronauts?"

"Yes! All of them. If that's where they placed their focus, every one of them could be anything. The only thing stopping them—" She cut herself off. Why was she going on about this?

"What could stop them?" Evan asked. "Who could?"

"Their neighborhood," she said. "We just had our budget voted down so we're on austerity. And austerity doesn't manifest a cutting-edge learning center. It manifests out-of-date textbooks and secondhand furniture and..." She stopped and took a breath. "Sorry. I get so annoyed."

"I can understand that seeing the kids not have everything they need for success would be very frustrating. Maybe you needed this long weekend away before school starts again?"

She looked at him for a moment. It was August. She'd normally be planning now for the upcoming year: buying supplies, going into school to prep and decorate her classroom. It was true she took a few days off from working this week, something she rarely did unless she was flat-out sick in bed. But she was confident about taking this time, confident that coming here would have a great end result, one that the kids would benefit from.

She didn't want to tell Evan, so she shifted the discussion back to him. "You said the race starts tomorrow night?"

He raised his brows. "Yes."

"Do you feel good about your chances? Are you just trying to finish or are you trying to win?"

He paused, and again, she was surprised at his honesty. Or modesty. Or both. "I—well," he began. "I'm confident I've trained the best I can. I never play to play. I always play to win. I'm not confident I'm at my athletic peak. That was a few years ago. I'm doing well for thirty-eight, but I've seen a bunch of the guys staying at this hotel, and they are a lot younger."

"Younger doesn't mean anything," Rachel said, maybe too quickly, because Evan's friendly gaze turned a little more studying.

She didn't want to give herself away now. She'd love the look on his face too much when he finally realized what he did wrong here.

"Younger doesn't mean anything," she repeated. "You said yourself that no one knows what this race involves, so you can't assume anyone has the advantage. Age-wise. Or anything else-wise." She cleared her throat. "It's probably just mindset. Everyone trying this is probably in pretty good shape. Those who aren't in as good shape will drop out early. And for those who are left, it's probably a big mental game. I'd guess that if you're being kept in the dark about what's involved, the race organizers love the idea of mentally breaking you with obstacles and tasks you don't expect."

"You sound like you know what you're talking about. Motivating kids into wanting to succeed has clearly given you insight into mindset."

"You think that's it, huh?"

"Well, I don't know much about you—"

"No, you don't," Rachel said.

"But I think it could be a good deduction, from what little I do know. Go ahead. Give me some advice. I promise I'll follow it."

"Wow, that's trusting," Rachel said.

"I think I have some good instincts every now and then."

And sometimes you don't, she thought. But hey, he was nice. He was trying to make a connection, and she appreciated that, at least. Though her lifelong instinct was to have the edge, to have the upper hand, she decided to throw him a bone.

"Here's my advice," she said. "Look at what's in front of you. Each time you get a surprise in this race—and it sounds like over two days you'll have a few—don't rush into it. It's a race, but take a minute or two to study, strategize, make a plan, and also a backup plan. Break any major task into smaller pieces. If you have to do one hundred pushups, think of it as five sets of twenty, which is way easier, right?"

Evan listened to her like she was Yoda, leaning toward her. He nodded his head slowly.

"Everything is not what you first think it is," she added. "Don't make assumptions. Really look at what's in front of you." She slid off the barstool. "Good luck. You'll kill it."

"Wait." He reached out to touch maybe her shoulder, but she backed up a few steps, so he touched air. "I like what you just said. I'd love to keep talking, if you want."

"I have to get up pretty early," Rachel said, with regret that surprised her.

"The race is over on Sunday..."

"Oh?"

"Yes. Maybe we can have dinner. If I'm not in an ice bath or on a gurney, of course. Will you still be here?"

"Oh, I'll still be here," she said. "Don't worry about that."

JENNIFER SAFREY

CHAPTER 2

Evan was certain the focus of meditation should not be the long chestnut hair of the woman he'd met the night before.

When his alarm went off, he slid to the floor beside his hotel bed. With his eyes opened to slits, he blindly fished the meditation cushion out of one of his backpacks. He settled it underneath him, set the timer on his phone, closed his eyes—and Rachel filled the space behind his eyelids.

That hair. Her eyes, wide and brown and fringed with extra-curly lashes. Her smile, crooked and somewhat knowing. Her body—in her oversized pink sweatshirt, not much was revealed. But her leggings clung tight to firm calves, her ankle socks in sneakers revealed delicately bare ankles, and her fingers damp with water-bottle condensation were graceful.

He shook his head. Inhale for four, hold the inbreath for four, exhale for four, hold the outbreath for four. In, hold, out, hold. Square breathing, meant to calm the mind, meant to slow the thoughts, meant to—

Rachel hadn't wanted to hang around. Had he done something wrong? It had been a long time since he'd talked to a pretty stranger in a hotel bar. No doubt, he was rusty, but once upon a time he had been pretty good at the art of conversation and flirtation. Had he gone that far south?

Breathe in for four, hold inbreath for four, breathe out for four—

Maybe it was supposed to be this way. Maybe he'd been meant to meet her and absorb her guru-like wisdom, and that was the part she was supposed to play in his life. He'd never put much stock in things like fate and destiny and meeting people for reasons and whatnot, but he'd also stopped putting stock in the idea that he knew anything about anything. Once you'd embarrassed yourself so badly and publicly that you had to leave your country to get some peace, you learned to take life as it came. You learned to take each breath as it came.

Breath. Right. Breathe in for four, hold for—

She was probably craving some alone time anyhow. That was why she came to this hotel. Or—he'd asked her why she came to this hotel and she hadn't really answered, had she? She hadn't. She'd told him a bit about her work, but other than that, he'd learned nothing about her. Not even her last name. He'd *had* to go on and on about the stupid race, didn't he? It was on his mind, after all. He was more than a little nervous about today and how things might go, but he was sure he'd asked her about herself a few times. Hadn't he? He should never try to make a connection with a woman right before a competition. He wasn't in any right mind.

Of course, he used to. He used to meet women the nights before matches and one activity didn't affect the other. But he was younger then. He wasn't an old athlete, trying to make a public comeback in a very strange kind of athletic event—more of a stunt.

Focus. Focus. Breathe. Slow thoughts, slow—

Meanwhile, in the midst of his short-lived attempt to talk to a woman, that woman had given him some incredible advice on focus. What had she said? Really look at what's in front of you. Don't rush. There's more to what you see than you think. Look deeper.

She was right. Football was not about pausing. He was running, running, running for an hour and a half. Following the ball, taking every split-second opportunity to make contact with it, making decisions more quickly than he possibly could off the pitch. He needed this particular advice because it wasn't something he was good at. Pausing. Reflecting. Making a plan. Making a plan B. Implementing that plan with precision.

Rachel had been absolutely right. It was a race, but taking those pauses would likely save a lot of stumbling and struggling later on. She must be an amazing teacher, inspiring. Her kids probably never gave up because she didn't give up on them.

He was glad *she* wasn't running The Golden Crucible. With that intuition and mindset, she'd be a formidable foe, despite her small size. And he needed to win.

He needed his comeback.

After Rachel had left last night, Evan had talked to a few guys hanging around the bar, competitors in this weekend's race. Many of them said they were doing it to see if they could. One man had lost 120 pounds in the last two years and was doing this to test how far he could get. One guy said he'd been running shorter obstacle races with some pals from work but he wanted to push the boundaries of his body. A few guys mentioned the prize money, higher than most races—seventy-five hundred dollars, which made sense as the entry fee was pretty steep.

Evan had been a professional athlete, and even he didn't know what he was getting into.

He felt his adrenaline flow. He took a deep, steadying breath. Oh, right. Breath. Breathe in—

The timer went off. Evan blew out hard through his mouth.

***

Gravel crunched under Evan's feet as he hopped out of the Uber. He waved at the driver and looked up the long dirt road. Even the uphill road leading to The Golden Crucible HQ appeared daunting. Evan started the ascent.

The race organizers had called the meeting for eight o'clock, to brief the racers on the rules and maybe give hints on what to expect. It was only seven fifteen, but Evan preferred to arrive extra early to get a feel for the people, the race, the general atmosphere.

The wind on his face was the opposite of cooling. The bold, bright New Hampshire summer sun wasn't the same shy sun in London, often hiding behind clouds and drizzle. He waved away a bee. A ceaseless insect buzzing surrounded him, the soundtrack of the woods of New England.

It was a steep hill and when Evan started to sweat a bit, it worried him. If climbing up one hill in the early-morning heat was an effort, he had no idea how he'd make it through forty-eight hours of grueling challenges. The packet he'd received in the mail last week had included a waiver to sign, acknowledging he knew the possibly fatal risks of this race. He'd smirked a bit upon signing it, knowing the drama was part of the experience. The closer it came to the start time, the more trepidation roiled in his stomach.

When he reached the top of the hill, he saw The Golden Crucible HQ wasn't an impressive, modern compound. It was a cluster of four log cabins, reminiscent of a sleepaway camp. They looked dark and quiet. A mini obstacle course lay beyond the furthest cabin. Since Evan was early and no one else seemed to be here for the meeting, he walked toward the course. Maybe he could squeeze in a quick warmup.

But someone *was* already there.

And that someone navigated the course with the ease of a ninja.

As Evan moved closer, he saw the person jump onto the first monkey bar and swing from one bar to the next smoothly, her body a pendulum moving in flawless time until the last bar.

Her body. Even from this distance and from behind, and with the person in generic shorts and T-shirt, he saw it was a woman.

She let go of the last bar and landed on the dirt, wiping her hands on her thighs. Then she jogged to the next obstacle, her long chestnut braid swinging back and forth.

Chestnut.

You mean climbing, jumping, stuff like that?

Look at what's in front of you.

Everything is not what you first think it is.

Oh, no. Oh, no.

What a colossal jerk he was.

What an unbelievable, stupid, and apparently sexist jerk he was.

Rachel jogged to an enormous truck tire on the ground, bent her knees to get a finger grip under the tread, and flipped it over. Once, twice. Then she ran in two long steps up a slanted six-foot wall, grabbed a frayed thick rope hanging over the top in one hand, hoisted herself up two more steps to the top, and disappeared behind it for a moment before circling back around it and doing twenty burpees without stopping. Twenty. He walked closer until he was a few feet away. Still, she didn't stop. Twenty times he watched her drop to the ground, do a full pushup, jump back up, and clap her hands in the air. She didn't pause, she didn't break. She did twenty and then bent to tie her sneaker lace without labored breath. When she stood, she saw him.

Now that he was closer, he saw what he'd missed last night: the muscle definition in her biceps, her triceps. Her thighs were hard, her calves sleek. Now that they were in the light of day, he noticed she had the all-over tan of a woman who spent her free time outside.

She looked at him. He opened his mouth to speak, shaking his head at the same time. He didn't know what to say first. *I'm so sorry I misjudged you. I'm sorry I never thought you could be one of the racers when this hotel is full of them. I'm sorry I made such a pathetic sexist mistake. I promise you my feminist mother would kill me because she didn't raise me to believe women were less than men. Maybe it's society's conditioning but apparently all men have some sexism to overcome and I'm so sorry that despite the fact I know I was awful, I'm still standing here wishing I knew what your body looks like under your shirt and...*

And she smiled at him.

It was the smile of a woman who knew exactly what regrets and apologies were on his tongue.

It was the smile of a woman who was pleased to have surprised him.

It was the smile of a woman who knew she was hot stuff, that she was in the best shape of her life, and if someone could possibly finish The Golden Crucible and finish it on top, it would be her.

"Good morning, Evan."

He lowered his gaze for a moment, then snorted out a laugh. "Good morning, Rachel." He glanced at the monkey bars. "At least you weren't politely lying to get out of talking to me last night. You did have to get up early."

"I never lie."

"Good to know." He cleared his throat. "So, I—"

She cut him off. "It's okay. Lots of men would have assumed the same thing. I just decided to have a little fun with you about it."

"I don't want to be 'lots of men.' I hold myself to a higher standard."

She seemed to think for a moment. "Good. Then consider it a lesson learned without much collateral damage."

He nodded.

"Is this the kind of stuff you trained?" she asked.

"Yeah," he said. "I've trained at a gym with this kind of equipment. I've done a few of the short obstacle races. Obviously you have as well."

"Yes, for a long time." She looked past him. "Here come

some people."

Evan turned and saw three men stepping onto the front porch of one of the cabins. Two of them carried boxes and clipboards. The third man unlocked the door, and they all went in.

"I guess we're about to find out what this is all about," Evan said.

"Yup." She walked past him toward the cabins, then turned. "Hey, I will accept that Sunday dinner invite as an apology. Somewhere fancy. But I won't want to be kept waiting because I'll need to drive back to Boston."

"Waiting?"

"Right. I'll be back to the hotel before you. Because I'm going to win."

Evan narrowed his eyes. "Is that so?"

"That's right."

She turned and walked away.

He bristled. So many trash-talk retorts fell from the recesses of his memory to his lips. But he bit them all back. He'd made enough of a fool of himself.

Besides, he knew from his old football days that in the end, trash-talking didn't mean anything. Performance did. Rachel had just given him the incentive he needed to grind out the best performance of his life.

"Hey," he called.

She turned.

"I really am sorry," he said.

Sorry I'll need to disappoint you. Sorry I have to win.

CHAPTER 3

About seventy athletes sprawled out on the long stretch of clover-covered grass behind one of the cabins, waiting for the powers that be to give them their mission. Rachel was happy she wasn't the only woman, but she saw only three others. They must have been staying at different hotels last night. Rachel wouldn't be able to carve out much opportunity to get to know them. Today would be a day for stretching, packing her gear, and strategizing based on what she was about to find out now.

She sneaked a look at Evan. A dozen men had grouped around him and were peppering him with questions, slapping him on the back, and laughing. Evan suddenly appeared to be in his element, grinning and gesturing. Mr. Personality. *Guess he made a lot of friends last night in the bar after I left.*

Sitting beside Rachel, a man with red hair and an unruly matching beard watched the group with interest. Rachel nudged him. "Wonder what they're so happy about."

The redhead nodded in their direction. "That's Evan Hughes."

Evan Hughes. Was that supposed to mean something to her? "Evan Hughes?"

"Yes, the soccer star? From England?"

Soccer star? "Like, professional soccer?"

"Oh, yeah," the redhead said. "Premier League. I'm surprised you don't know who he is."

"I don't watch soccer."

"But even if you don't, he's famous, like David Beckham famous. Guess you don't read the tabloids."

She didn't. She wasn't into celebrity news and gossip, didn't have much time for movies and TV. She taught weekdays, brought grading and lesson plans home for evenings, and raced or trained on weekends. Summers were for longer outdoor adventures. By the looks of the men falling all over Evan—and by his physical looks—he was definitely a star.

Everything is not what you first thought, all right. The joke was on her, after all.

"Why is he here?" she wondered aloud.

"He fell off the radar," the redhead told her. "He retired a few years ago, had a big breakup with some model chick, and then he kind of vanished. Didn't know he was in the US."

Rachel's mind went into turbo mode. If this guy was a professional soccer player not too long ago, what did he bring to the table for this race? She didn't recognize any other racers here, and that made sense, because elite obstacle-course racers like herself disregarded The Golden Crucible. She'd met all the top podium men and women— she was one of them. They considered The Golden Crucible an unserious stunt race. Not something you could train for because you didn't know what would be thrown at you. Dangerous, unpredictable, and stupid. A relatively new franchise and not an officially sanctioned race. Just a race that somewhat above-average weekend athletes ran to prove something to themselves psychologically. And they were mostly correct. It was an event for daredevils, ne'er-do-wells, and normal people who wanted to be jolted from their everyday desk lives. Not serious athletes. Rachel figured that with her racing pedigree, she'd be a, if not *the*, top contender for the big cash prize. Most of the respected obstacle-course races didn't offer as much in prize money as The Golden Crucible. The one that did, the Prestige Race, had four times as many athletes in the race as this did. Many of them elite, with a legitimate shot at winning.

But a professional soccer player might bring something else to this renegade event. He was likely an excellent distance runner. Those soccer players could go for ninety-plus minutes, often at top speed. Evan's endurance would be superior. He'd have way-above-average reflexes and reaction times. But even if he'd trained for a year or two, he wouldn't have Rachel's many years of expertise on equipment, her grip strength, and her ability to navigate obstacles with speed.

He wouldn't need to win, not the way she did. She had lost the Prestige Race six months ago and decided to enter The Golden Crucible for a chance at similar prize money. She had that prize money earmarked for the highest good. That was all the motivation in the world. This win wouldn't be for a medal or a few podcast appearances for niche obstacle-course racing fans. It would be for the kids. It was her best chance to give them something other than you-can-do-it speeches and pats on the back.

Ugh, now Evan Hughes stood right in her path.

She really wished she hadn't given him some pretty good mindset advice the day before. But she'd thought he was an average racer, just a guy who was hitting on her. She didn't know he'd be the likely one to beat. Again, the joke was on her. While he was underestimating her as a woman, she'd been unwittingly busy underestimating him as a man.

Sigh. She should have known. Her whole life, any time she'd made a connection to a man—romantically, as colleagues, as anything—she'd ended up in some kind of competition, some kind of one-upmanship with him. Instead of playing an amusing game in her mind last night with him, she should have been sizing him up, asking him questions about himself and his experience.

Instead, she'd been distracted by his charm and his pretty—seriously, *beyond* pretty—face.

A rookie mistake. One she couldn't afford to make again in the next few days.

A salt-and-pepper-haired man in a navy-blue polo shirt carried a clipboard as he walked to the front of the group and whistled loudly. Everyone quieted down and sat on the grass and on the big boulders scattered around. When Rachel glanced at Evan, he was looking at her. She raised her eyebrows, then slid from her perch on a boulder to the grass. Her butt was getting sore.

"Competitors," the man started. "I'm Justin Roberts, the creator of The Golden Crucible. I'm here to tell you a bit about what you're in for." He held up the clipboard. "Did anyone not sign a waiver?"

No response.

"Good." He tucked it under his arm. "You're all here for one reason: to win. I'd like to say one of you will win. More likely, none of you will finish and I can keep the prize money for myself. Do you see what's happening here? I designed this course to make it very difficult for you to pry seven thousand, five hundred dollars from my grip. I don't want to give you money. I want to buy stuff for myself. That's where I'm coming from when I design this course. Got it?"

Okay, the psych-out started right here. Rachel nodded slowly. This was a mind game, and she was above mind games. She knew why she was here and why she wanted to win. She saw the mind games for exactly what they were. Some other racers, however, shifted uncomfortably.

"So," Justin continued, "if you think I'm going to stand here like an idiot and tell you all what you'll face for the next two and a half days, you can forget it. Here's what I will tell you. Dress for frigid temperatures. And scorching heat. Bring food and water because I may or may not decide to feed you guys. If I do, it will be on a schedule I determine."

Rachel had fully predicted this unpredictability.

"If you are not physically able to complete a challenge or an obstacle, or if you strongly suspect you can't before you try, you must quit," Justin went on. "Next. You are required to take a six-hour break for rest-slash-sleep every twenty-four hours during this race. If twenty-four consecutive hours have elapsed without you taking that six-hour break, you will be eliminated. We will find you on the course and remove you. Six hours. I've had too many morons try to run this race straight without rest. That's a recipe for injury or illness for you, and a recipe for liability for me. So, breaks are enforced."

Rachel was surprised but pleased with this built-in safety measure.

"Now," Justin said, "in case you're thinking of kicking back with a mai-tai and a stack of *Cosmo* magazines, allow me to inform you that if you take fifteen minutes longer than those six hours, we will assume you have dropped out and, again, we will find you and take you off the course. You have unlimited opportunities to take breaks of a half-hour or less, in case you need to tie your shoes or have water or change your clothes or pray to your God of choice that the race ends soon. But this is still a race, so maybe keep your breaks to a minimum. I will have people all over this course monitoring every single one of you with a cuff you'll wear on your ankle. Not one of you will be off the grid. You'll also have a button on the cuff that you can press and we can send help to you immediately. If we send help, you can't then decide you're fine. If you ask for help for any reason, you must quit. You're done."

His face softened just a bit. "We don't want you to be hurt or dead at the end of this event. We only want you to push, try your best, and dig deep. If you have to drop out, you'll be in good company. Most do. Then you come back here to HQ and hang out and cheer the rest of the racers on and we'll have a party at the end."

The redhead Rachel had been talking to raised his hand. "Can we help each other?"

"It's not against the rules to help each other," Justin said. "You can do whatever you want. You can form teams, I don't care. But in the end, a team doesn't win. An individual does. There's no second-place prize. If you're in it to the end, and you want to be the winner, at some point you have to put yourself first, yeah? Okay." He slid the clipboard out from under his arm and glanced at it again. "I'm going to call out names to make sure everyone is here. You wouldn't be surprised that every time, a handful of people pay the entry fee and then don't have the balls to show up."

Rachel felt Evan slide next to her on the grass. She tried not to look at him. "Want to be a team?" he asked.

She stared at him. "Why would I want to do that? So I'd help you the whole race and then have to beat you in the last fifty yards? And why didn't you tell me you're a famous soccer player?"

"We call it football where I'm from. And I'm not anymore. Maybe it would have come up if you hung around longer to talk to me."

"I think you've found plenty of people to talk to."

"When I call your name," Justin said, "get up here for your cuff and your number."

"They only want to talk about football," Evan said.

"We call it soccer where I'm from," Rachel said.

"Besides," Evan added, "I need to concentrate on what's happening here."

"Rachel Bowen!"

She hopped up and went over to Justin's assistant. He used a thick black marker to write her race number on the skin of her upper arm. Then he handed her the marker and asked her to write the same number as large as she could on her thigh. As she did, he knelt to secure her ankle cuff. He showed her how to adjust the cuff for comfort, then demonstrated how it worked. "You press this blue button to turn the cuff on," he said. "Turn it on five minutes before the start of the race and don't turn it off at all until the race is over or until you—"

"I won't."

"Right," he said. "And press this red button if you need medical or any other kind of help." Then he held out a wooden box. "Your cell phone."

"You're taking my phone? Now?"

"Yes."

Rachel slid it out of her shorts pocket and placed it in the box. She watched as he peeled a label with her name on it off a sheet and stuck it across the back of her phone. "You'll get it back at the end of the race or if you—"

"I won't."

"Right," he said.

She went back to her spot on the grass, where the redhead asked Evan about some goal in some game in some European country at some point in time.

"Evan Hughes!"

The group went silent as Evan stood. Justin watched him for maybe an extra second before returning his attention to his list. Rachel was glad to see Evan was being treated like anyone else. She definitely understood that Evan's presence could be a big thing for Justin and his race event. The race didn't enjoy a lot of respect. Though the number of competitors was solid, it wasn't particularly impressive. If she was Justin, she'd be looking to somehow give his race more notoriety. If Evan Hughes was the celebrity he seemed to be, that would bring attention.

Not that Rachel wanted the attention. She'd prefer the OCR community not know she was running this disrespected race. She wouldn't have bothered if not for her piss-poor performance the last time in competition. This was her revenge race, and her only other chance at a decent cash prize until next year.

"Hughes!" called a voice. "Hey, Evan Hughes!"

Rachel, Evan, and the entire group looked up to see a man about a hundred yards away, holding up a big sign that said GO HUGHES! in Sharpie. He waved a huge red foam number-one finger with his other hand. He wore a short-sleeved red-and-white striped jersey, but the sleeve holes gaped over his elbows and the rest of the shirt hung slack around his slight torso. His hair was cropped short. Rachel put him between the ages of eighteen and forty-nine. Enthusiastic men in pro sports garb looked like thrilled little boys and it was impossible to tell.

The man, seeing he had the attention of the group, sang a crazy song at the top of his lungs. She couldn't make out the words, but he pumped his fist to the staccato notes at the end of each phrase. Without knowing the song, she could tell he was way off key. A bunch of the racers clapped in time. She looked at Evan. He didn't seem embarrassed or flustered. When the fan got to the last line, Evan called it out with him, adding his own punctuating fist pumps. The racers cheered. Justin sent one of his clipboard guys over to chase the fan away. "You got this, Hughes!" the man called. "Beat these chumps!"

"Hey!" a few of the racers called, offended after their show of support. One halfheartedly threw an empty juice box at the fan as he and his foam finger and his sign were shooed down the hill away from the group.

Rachel pretended to examine her cuff so someone else could engage Evan in conversation. Someone did, very quickly, then another and another, until he was once again at the center of a circle of male admirers.

She didn't want to risk liking him. After she won, maybe that would be a different story. Maybe he'd still want dinner.

Once the last racer went up to collect his cuff and number, Justin said, "All right, folks. Race starts tonight at six p.m. You have most of the day free. Get your butts right back in this spot no later than five forty-five. Before you go, we'll move this meeting to the conference room in the main cabin. Let's go."

Not giving anyone time to ask why, he turned and headed toward the main cabin, his two staff guys following him. Everyone looked confused as to why they were not yet dismissed. Rachel stood, brushed grass off her rear end, and joined the group trudging to the cabin.

Evan fell in step beside her. "How are you planning to prep today?" he asked.

Rachel hesitated, but she wouldn't be revealing any state secrets if she told him the truth. "Sleeping, mostly," she confessed. "Stretching. Eating whatever they give us for lunch. Packing my gear. Chasing away my devoted fans with signs and songs to cheer me on. You?"

He looked embarrassed. "About the same."

"I want to get started on all that now, though," Rachel said. "I wonder what we're doing first."

They reached the cabin's front door, and the man in front of them held it open. Evan took it and waved Rachel in. The fresh wood smell reminded her of camp. The floorboards creaked comfortably under her trail sneakers. All the walls held glass showcases filled with The Golden Crucible photos. The happiest photos were the group "before" photos—mostly men but some women with arms around one another, clean clothes, wide smiles, relaxed bodies. The other photos, action photos, depicted more harrowing moments: racers slithering on their bellies through mud underneath barbed wires, racers staggering under buckets filled to the brim with rocks, racers clutching tree trunks while climbing hills with practically vertical inclines, and racers lying on the dry, dusty ground, staring at the sky, the looks on their faces ranging from fatigue to regret to defeat. On a far wall were photos of racers wearing medals, but not many. Even those racers didn't look okay, as if holding in a massive vomit session or long cry until after the photo was taken.

Again, a psych-out. Rachel was sure the staff had decided to walk the group by these photos in an effort to put a good scare into them. Rachel had had tough races before. She'd thrown up during and after races. She'd borne uncomfortable weight, pushed through mud, and trudged up sharp inclines before. She could do this. The one wild card was not knowing the obstacles ahead of time. She just had to be adaptable. As each challenge was presented, she'd make a plan, and a plan B. This was doable. Everything was doable.

She was secretly pleased many of the men around her eyed the photos with alarm on their faces. Some were too cocky to look. Fear and cockiness usually had the same flattening result.

Evan had drifted in front of her at some point. She couldn't see him, and she tried not to look for him.

They emerged into a sizable room with folding chairs lined along the walls. A table was set up front with five chairs and five microphones. A half-dozen rows of chairs stood in the center of the room. Justin instructed the racers to sit in the chairs along the perimeter of the room.

Rachel looked around the space for more of a clue. Would they listen to guest speakers of some kind? But who would sit in the center? What was going on?

When all the athletes were seated, the doors opened and in streamed—the press.

The press?

The legitimate sports press. Reporters with notebooks, cameramen lugging equipment, and photographers.

What the—? Rachel looked at the reporters' microphones and saw logos for major sports networks. She squinted at name badges and saw a few newspapers and well-known sports blogs. It was no White House briefing-room crowd, but fifteen reporters had come, fifteen more than Rachel had ever seen at any of her past races.

When everyone was seated, Evan stood and took a seat at the front table. He turned the microphone toward him, flicked a switch, and tapped the mic with his finger.

Of *course.* Of course. Justin, no fool, had called a press conference to drum up interest in his race with his star entrant.

This wasn't fair. In no way. It wasn't fair to the other racers to turn this into a one-celebrity show and make them watch it. Rachel was torn between stalking from the room and taking a nap to forget this—forget Evan—and staying to see if she could capitalize on anything Evan revealed about his training, his strategy, anything.

Justin introduced himself to the room of reporters, gave a brief history of The Golden Crucible and what it involved, and then introduced Evan Hughes, their most famous racer to date. Then he stepped aside.

"Evan! Evan!" the reporters called.

Evan cleared his throat. "I'm chuffed to be a part of The Golden Crucible this year. It's a unique event, and as soon as I heard of it, I wanted to be a part of it. As some of you know, I used to play a bit of football." Everyone chuckled. "Well, soccer, you call it. Football has many rules. You learn them, and you become the best you can in accordance with those rules within the confines of a match. You do your best, but you can't do anything you want, because you'll get a yellow card or a dreaded red card. You learn to react within the rules to any crazy thing that happens, any direction the ball comes from.

"I retired from the sport because I played a long time. I was tired of getting injured. It was time to give younger players their chance. And I was ready to move to the next phase in my life. But that doesn't mean I don't want a challenge. My good friend in the States told me about this race, and it seemed like something I needed to remind myself that I'm still tough and competitive. I don't think I'll make a career of this, but it's time to do something different and a little shocking to my system. Thank you all for coming here and giving the race some publicity, but other athletes in this race deserve attention. I see some other chairs up here for them. I hope you'll give them that attention now."

The room erupted with questions. "Evan! You've been underground for a while ever since your split with Grace Regan two years ago. Is this your public comeback?"

Grace Regan?

Who was Grace Regan?

Evan smiled a bit crookedly. "This has nothing to do

with Grace, whom I wish all the best. Maybe I intend this race to be a bit of a public comeback, but an athletic one."

"Maybe a win would get her attention?"

"I'm not looking to get her attention," Evan said, an edge to his voice.

Rachel had no idea whether to be empathetic or fascinated. She wouldn't want people asking her about a breakup from two years ago. In romance, that was a lifetime and one became a different person in that amount of time. But damn if she wasn't pissed her phone had been taken away so she couldn't Google Grace Regan.

A few other reporters asked about Grace. Evan only shook his head. Another reporter, sensing that line of questioning was over, tried a different tack. "How have you trained for this race? Have you even trained, and what do you think your strengths are as a competitor?"

Evan seemed relieved. "Thanks, mate, for asking. I think my reflexes are sharp. I can see what's coming at me in all directions, I'm used to going for a while without stopping, and I handle pressure well. You have to when thousands of football fans are wishing for your demise at the same time thousands are cheering you on. I've been in New England almost two years, staying with my best mate. I've had the opportunity to train on the terrain here and in all kinds of weather. I think I'm ready to compete."

He cleared his throat again. "As I said, I think it's time to give the other racers some due."

These reporters would never be interested in anyone else here. It wasn't possible. But Justin was at the front of the room, saying, "We went through the racers' applications and picked out whom we think are the other four top favorites going in, based on their experience and pedigrees."

What were they, thoroughbreds?

He rattled off their names and called them up to the table to have a seat. The selected men looked as shocked as Rachel felt to suddenly have media attention on this race. To have anyone other than their families caring about the outcomes this weekend. They seemed to squirm as a group while their accomplishments were listed—accomplishments they had been asked to list on their application when prompted: *What qualifies you as a top contender for The Golden Crucible?* The qualifications included not only races but other athletic pursuits, and impressive business and personal achievements.

"Last, but not least," Justin said, "we round out our top five with Rachel Bowen."

She didn't move. The reporters looked at the few women in the room.

Rachel had wanted to run this race in obscurity. She hadn't wanted to explain it to others in her sport later. She hadn't wanted her kids to find out and get their hopes up for her. She'd wanted to win quietly and present the money to the school.

But Evan looked at her. The reporters eventually followed his gaze. She sighed and rose from her chair, then walked woodenly to the last chair at the end of the head table. She sat, and the man to her right helpfully turned her microphone on. Justin listed her most recent qualifications for the media: two-time winner of the Dynamic Diamond Race, winner of the Summer Summit Challenge, second-place finisher at the Ever-Elite Event, and fourth place at the Prestige Race. The last race was the reason Rachel was here, the one for which she'd counted on prize money and lost.

Photographers snapped her picture. She didn't know in which direction to look. She wished she wasn't here. She wished she was anywhere else but here.

***

Halfway across the table, Evan sensed her discomfort. He wasn't sure why. She was getting mainstream recognition those in her sport rarely got. And she'd been pretty confident earlier in her stated intent to win.

"Does anyone have any questions?" Justin asked the room.

"Evan! Evan—"

Evan held up a hand. "No more for me, please. You can direct your questions to my fellow competitors."

"Rachel! Rachel!"

Because she was different, because she was a woman, the reporters turned to her. A female reporter said, "Rachel, how do you feel about this race?"

"I feel the same way I feel about every race," she said, her voice steady. "I feel that if I put in my best race, I'll win."

"It was only last year that the first woman finished The Golden Crucible," another reporter said. "Though she didn't win. How do you feel about that?"

Rachel hadn't actually known that. "She was obviously amazing, and I plan to be amazing too."

"Do you feel like your age is a disadvantage?" called out a young male reporter.

Evan winced. A sudden hush fell over the room.

"My age?" Rachel repeated, her expression neutral.

"Yes," the reporter said. "According to my deep Google research"—he held up his phone—"you're forty-five. Do you feel like your age puts you at a disadvantage?"

Rachel waited a beat. "How old are you?"

The reporter hesitated, and Rachel added, "Come on. You told this whole room my age. Fair is fair. How old are you?"

"Twenty-six."

"Twenty-six," Rachel repeated. "Tell you what. Why don't you come up here and arm wrestle me? See for yourself if my age is a disadvantage."

"Oooooooo," all the people in the room chorused. The reporter's face flushed pink. Evan tried not to laugh.

"No?" Rachel asked. "Anyone else want to make an issue out of my age? Or anyone else's age? Certainly I'm not the oldest person in this race. Yet I'm the one asked. I can't imagine why."

Eyes down, the reporter shook his head, either in embarrassment or frustration. Evan shifted in his seat. Should he say something? No, Rachel was handling it. He didn't want to appear as though he was trying to rescue her. She didn't need it. If these reporters had seen the way she moved her body on the equipment outside—Evan shifted again. *Stop thinking about Rachel's body. Just stop.*

Fortunately, Justin stood and held up his hand. "I want to let all the racers get their rest, but the last thing we need to do is promote our sponsor. Our sponsor this year—our first year with a sponsor—is Magnitude Sports Drink." He consulted his clipboard. "Uh, 'Destroy your weakness with Magnitude.' Okay. Magnitude sent some gear for our top five contenders to wear."

A man and a woman in Magnitude tank tops jumped up from the corner of the room, pumped their fists with enthusiasm, and yelled, *"Magnitude!"* Evan held back a wince. The man reached into a shopping bag and pulled out a shirt and shorts, and the woman ran over to Evan and handed them to him with a giggle. Evan shook them out. The black nylon shorts were just right. The shirt was a red short-sleeved rash guard with the Magnitude logo in gold on the front, and HUGHES on the back. It was a slick shirt. Evan had wanted to wear his own gear, but he knew the importance of sponsors, so he smiled. "Nice. Thanks so much."

The Magnitude reps gave out the rest of the outfits. The men at the table unfolded their shirts and smiled. Evan could see they enjoyed the elite-athlete treatment, and they should. They had good records that got them to this table, and this was unexpected for them.

When the rep approached Rachel, she said, "Yours is a little different," and gave her two scraps of material. Rachel frowned and unfolded them. A red sports bra with the gold Magnitude logo, and the smallest pair of red spandex shorts Evan had ever seen that weren't actually underwear. The bra had BOWEN down the racer back in fairly small font, since there wasn't enough material for it to be any larger.

Rachel said, "Thank you." Her expression was hard to read. If she was embarrassed, she hid it well. Maybe it was disappointment that spread her lips thin, or anger. Evan couldn't tell, but he was disappointed for her and angry on her behalf. From her short performance on the equipment earlier and the list of accolades he'd heard from Justin, it was clear she deserved to be here. What she didn't deserve was to be dressed differently, singled out for being female.

Evan pulled the microphone toward him and said, "There appears to be some mistake. I think Rachel got my outfit."

Everyone laughed. Rachel stared at him for a moment before she relented. Her smile, even this small one, was radiant. He tossed her his T-shirt, and she pulled it over her head. She tossed him the sports bra and he hung it around his neck. Then he stood and went over to her. He bent over her chair and put his arm around her shoulders. She blinked in surprise, then slid her arm under his, wrapping it around his back. They grinned for the video cameras.

Evan was glad for the cameras and reporters, a distraction from Rachel's warm, strong body enveloped in his arm.

"Her versus Him," one of the racers sitting at the wall called out.

Rachel kept smiling, but Evan felt her stiffen ever so slightly.

CHAPTER 4

Evan escaped the conference room at lunchtime. The Golden Crucible provided lunch for the racers in the main cabin's cafeteria, so Evan heaped a tray high with a burger, cottage cheese, and salad. Lots of protein and veg. Who knew when he'd have his next meal? He had a feeling Justin might make them suffer this evening with little to no dinner, so Evan served himself enough food to fuel him through race time. He'd stash a ton of protein bars in his pack.

Rachel sat alone at one of the long tables. Evan slid in next to her.

"What are you doing?" she asked. "In the big story of Her versus Him, eating lunch with me would be considered consorting with the enemy."

"Having a burger together is hardly trying to elicit classified secrets from you," he pointed out and took a messy bite. He wiped his mouth, noticing at least as much food was on her tray, the same kind of protein-and-veg fest.

"That was insane," he said conversationally.

"What was?"

"Reporters."

"Like you didn't know they'd be here. Like you didn't set it all up."

"Yeah, I did know, but I didn't set it up," he said. "It was all Justin's doing. I didn't know it was happening until yesterday. Justin asked if I minded, and I said no. I've done tons of these. It was nice that I wasn't the only one being interviewed, though. But if I win—"

She snorted, and he wished she hadn't.

"If I win," he continued, "I figure I can use the publicity to get back on the media radar. I'm ready to make a comeback. A win would help get me back in the spotlight as a viable athlete. I wasn't interested in attention before I ran, but Justin asked and it's good for his business. But I don't love the pre-competition pressure, in case things don't go as well as I plan."

"*You* don't need that kind of pressure?" Rachel shoved her mouth full of food, almost as a deliberate effort to try to measure her words. "You know who doesn't need this pressure? Anyone else in the race. Most of all, me. Since they are really interested in me now. No one else at the top of obstacle-course racing takes The Golden Crucible seriously. They say it's dangerous, stupid, and sullies the reputation of good obstacle-course racers as daredevils and stunt people instead of athletes. I've worked hard to be at the top of my game. I didn't want—"

She cut herself off and took a long sip of water, then sat there glowering at him.

"Didn't want what?" he eventually prompted.

"I didn't want anyone to know I'm doing this race. I wanted to keep it quiet. Even if I won, The Golden Crucible is a weird underground event for thrill-seekers, not a legit race. No one would have found out. Now, it could very well be prime time. At least on the sports pages. That's fine for you. But suddenly I'm the woman—and not only that, but an apparently over-the-hill woman—with the audacity to try to beat professional athlete Evan Hughes, every man's crush."

"Hey," he said.

"Oh, my God, like you don't know that. Like that guy

with his homemade sign didn't come from who-knows-where to cheer you on. Like every guy all morning hasn't been falling over themselves to hold your water bottle."

"Is that what we're calling it now?"

She stared at him.

"Sorry," he muttered. "Just trying to lighten the mood."

"Also," Rachel said, "I've been thinking this whole time you're modest and—but you're not, are you? Agreeing to this attention pre-race means deep down, you think you'll win or at least get very close."

Evan went silent. She knew that under his spoken trepidation was confidence. He was sure that as a former pro athlete, his half effort would be better than others' full efforts. Maybe he wasn't wrong, in terms of the majority of the racers. He was counting on it. But maybe he shouldn't.

"Now I'm the co-headliner in Her versus Him," she added. "And if you think that won't gain traction on social media—"

"What if it does?" he asked. "Okay, I understand you're here and you didn't want anyone to know that you're here. But, false modesty aside, I'm a famous footballer, if a bit of a has-been. And I'm in the race. Don't you think that would change the minds of the top people in your racing circles about this event? Maybe they'll be sorry they weren't here too, to get a chance for fame by kicking my ass?"

"I highly doubt it. And it's not just that," Rachel said. "I don't—I didn't want my students to know."

"Why not? How would it not benefit your students to see their math and science teacher is a badass? More than that—a badass *woman*? A superheroine?"

"I just—this isn't exactly a risk I'd encourage them to take. Running this race isn't the smartest thing you and I could be doing with our time. But you have your reason to run it, and I have mine."

"What is yours?" he asked, taking another bite of his burger. After he swallowed, he said, "You don't strike me as someone who needs a thrill or a jolt out of her everyday life.

A lot of the guys here, that's what they need. Or they want a good story to tell at the pub. You, though, you seem to have a fulfilling career, something you care about full time, something to get you out of bed in the morning." He scooped up cottage cheese with a plastic spoon and made himself eat it. Cottage cheese was revolting but packed with protein. "You already race very successfully. Is it the cash prize? It can't be that much higher than other races you've run."

Rachel shook her head. "Not that I owe you an explanation, but most races like this don't offer big prize money. There's only one a year that offers $10,000. That was two months ago. I came in fourth."

"So you signed up for The Golden Crucible for a chance at a cash prize because otherwise, you'd need to wait a year to try again."

She didn't nod but she didn't indicate he was wrong. She bit into a green apple and looked around the room.

"The money must be important to you. Why?"

"Listen," she said. "I appreciate your going to bat for me earlier about my special skimpy outfit from the sponsor. I really do. You did me a solid. Most guys not only wouldn't have bothered, but wouldn't have noticed it was an issue to dress me differently. But I don't want to share hopes and dreams with you. I need to beat you. And I need to beat everyone else here, including three guys sitting with us at that table today who I learned aren't slouches at life. So maybe we can eat without talking."

They crunched for a while, Rachel working her way around the apple core and Evan forking salad into his mouth. Finally, he asked her, "Are you going to wear it?"

She sighed. "I was going to wear something similar anyway. I like as much of my body free as possible. I have cold-weather gear for later, but while it's warm, it's best to wear something small that won't make me overheat and will dry quickly if I end up in water. Before, it was my choice. When the sponsor gave us these—" She shook her head.

"It wasn't your choice anymore," Evan finished for her. She nodded.

"I get it," he said.

"We have to, though, don't we?" she asked.

"I'm afraid so. At least for part of the race. The sponsor pays for placement on you."

"That's fine. It'll be covered in mud and sweat after about two hours anyway."

"If you're trying to knock me off my game by talking about you sweaty and covered in mud, it won't work."

Rachel looked at him, expressionless.

"I'm just kidding. I mean, it would definitely work."

She rolled her eyes. "Just when I thought you were Team Feminist."

"I thought you didn't want to be a team."

"Look." She wiped her mouth indelicately and tossed her napkin and apple core on her now-empty plate. "I have no reason not to like you. It's not personal. You're doing what you have to do to make this race work for you. So am I. That makes us rivals. Most races I want to win, and I usually do. This race, I have to win."

He nodded slowly. He tried to hide how Rachel blew his mind, as a human being, as an athlete, and as a woman. She was tough. She was gorgeous. She was take-no-prisoners. She was determined. And she was his enemy—for the next two and a half days.

If he beat her, he suspected he'd be her enemy long past two and a half days.

He put out his hand. "Then may the best runner win."

Rachel put her hand in his. He instantly wished he hadn't offered to shake. He should have remembered how she'd felt in his arms when their pictures were taken.

Before he could figure out how to squelch down his uncomfortably growing attraction, Rachel slid out of her chair and took her tray away.

JENNIFER SAFREY

CHAPTER 5

Rachel should have been in the middle of a very long, restorative nap. She'd already asked the front desk to give her a wake-up call. That wake-up call was due to happen in less than an hour, and was she getting sleep? No. She'd tried for forty-five minutes to fall asleep, but she'd slept a lot the night before. Her body wasn't having it in the middle of the day. Was she instead spending the time packing her cold-weather layers, her protein bars and energy gels, her mustard packets, her water pack belt, her first-aid kit, her sunscreen, her anything? No. She sat in front of her laptop, scrolling through pages of Google results on one Evan Hughes.

Very useful and productive.

She'd told herself it was a reconnaissance mission on her strongest competitor. But the pictures of Evan and Grace Regan at a nightclub in their best night-clubby clothes weren't likely to give Rachel any insight on how to beat him. It provided insight on the type of woman he liked to spend time with.

That type was, in a word, *perfect*. Grace Regan, a model-slash-actress, possessed every appropriate attribute a model-slash-actress should, in excess: the flawless skin of a Christmas tree-topper angel figurine, legs as long and reedy as a baby thoroughbred's, and a smile full of straight, shiny white Chiclets. Although her modeling wasn't in world-class publications and her acting wasn't in A-list movies, her distant-cousin relation to Princess Kate Middleton and her fall-down-dead appearance made her a beloved star in Great Britain. Evan and Grace—or Gravan, as the annoying-as-hell tabloids dubbed them—were luminous in every picture in every venue: award shows, World Cup events, and swanky restaurants. One photo showed Evan and Grace walking on the street, pretending to be mortal, him holding a takeout coffee cup and her sporting a yoga mat bag slung across her torso. Her hair looked unkempt and windblown and ridiculously perfect. How? How did goddesses like this exist?

But at the top of the Google search were the articles and the photos of their breakup. Articles showing grainy black-and-white photos of Grace looking pained and teary, splashed with big headlines like *EVAN CRUSHES GRACE'S HEART* and *GRACE REGAN: I'll BE OK ONE DAY, I HOPE* and *EVAN HUGHES OUT ON THE TOWN; GRACE HOLED UP AT HOME.*

Rachel didn't read the lurid stories under the headlines. Maybe she would after The Golden Crucible. At this moment, it felt like an unfair advantage for her to know the details of his lowest of low points when he didn't know much about her at all.

Despite her refusal to pore over every word of the celebrity rags' gossip, two things were patently clear: she wasn't Evan Hughes's type, and if she was, she'd be in for the heartbreak of the century without an entire nation supporting her in a time of sorrow the way they supported the gorgeous cousin of the beloved princess.

Not that Rachel was interested in being Evan Hughes's girlfriend. Just … good information to know.

She hit the *back* button to the Google search bar and typed, *Evan Hughes soccer career.*

It was a hit on thousands of pages. Rachel went down

another rabbit hole of videos of Hughes scoring goals, videos of interviews before and after matches, and videos of late-night TV appearances. After a while of watching his handsome mouth smile at show hosts and witnessing his strong arms held aloft as he ran across the field after a goal, Rachel tried to do some real recon.

She noticed Evan had a propensity for earning yellow cards—so she gathered he was a rule bender and a boundary pusher if he thought he could get away with it. This was good to know for the next few days. He was aggressive, taking every advantage to show soccer was a contact sport with tackling, pushing, and shoving—earning those yellow cards but apparently being fine with earning penalties as long as he took an opponent out of stride. He was bossy, shouting and gesturing at his teammates constantly, but one could call that motivating his team to perform their best.

Performing his best—that was what Evan seemed to do. Rachel knew the rudimentary rules of soccer and admittedly was familiar with none of the nuance. From what she saw, Evan left one hundred percent of himself on the field in every match.

He'd retired two years ago. But there was no reason to believe he'd left that quality behind, bringing one hundred percent of himself into his work.

It was hot.

And it was a warning to any athlete who went up against him.

The blast of the hotel phone ring almost sent Rachel through the ceiling. She wasn't nervous by nature, but who even heard a landline phone ring anymore? She picked it up and heard the recording. "This is your wake-up call. This is your wake-up call. This is—"

She put the phone back on the receiver with a clatter and glanced at the bedside clock. One hour until showtime.

Her father and her brothers likely had been blowing up her cell phone with good-luck and you-can-do-it texts, but The Golden Crucible had taken her phone. She wouldn't see them until after the race.

Normally, she enjoyed the adrenaline flooding her veins right before a race. It was like a booster shot of kick-ass that she could use as fuel. Today, though, the nervousness didn't feel good. It felt less like anticipation and excitement and an awful lot more like dread.

Not dread for the race itself. She liked a challenge, and she enjoyed the mystery behind what they'd be asked to do. What she didn't like was that she'd be a headline later if this was a slow news day. She didn't like that Evan Hughes had put her there. She didn't like that Evan Hughes was sexy and cute and kind of sweet. She had to remember he was a warrior on game day and a heartbreaker on the weekend. She didn't have room for either of those things, no matter how holy-hell *hot* he was.

She checked all the compartments in her backpack, filled all her water packs, and set about zipping and snapping the whole thing up. Then she slid her arms into the backpack and hoisted it up. A little heavier than she'd have liked, but her consumption of water and snacks would lighten the load as time went on. She tossed the bag back on the bed. She slid her hotel key card into a Ziploc baggie and secured it in a watertight compartment in her pack.

She yanked the Magnitude bra top and shorts off the bed, glared at them, and peeled off her clothes. Then she looked in the mirror above the dresser. Grace Regan, she was not. Not even close. Her body wasn't lithe and delicate as a baby bird. Her hair was thick and unruly. She liked her body, she really did. She'd worked hard for this body, and more than how it looked, she liked how it could do things. Things she couldn't do when she was twenty-five, or thirty-five. She'd only been an athlete for the last ten years, and it had transformed her inside and out.

She put on the outfit and packed what she'd been wearing. It was nice to have scored an extra outfit, even if the way she'd received it was embarrassing. She pulled on her socks and pushed her feet into her trail sneakers, which used to be a cool purple/orange combo but were now caked with several races' worth of mud and dirt. She'd cleaned and dried the insides several times, but there was no restoring them to their original shiny condition. She'd worn them when she dominated the Dynamic Diamond Race. She'd worn them when she tanked the Prestige Race. Rachel didn't harbor any sentimental attachment or lucky feelings to her gear. She used what she liked best.

She shrugged her bag onto her back again. Go time.

Rachel went to the hotel lobby and called an Uber. None of the racers were in the lobby, but she wasn't surprised. She was running about forty-five minutes early because she liked to be the first one there. First one there, first one done on Sunday. She liked being first.

The Uber dropped her off at the bottom of the long gravel drive and she trudged up slowly, conserving her energy. When she got to the top, she saw Evan.

He didn't see her, though.

She had come up on his right. He sat on a large boulder behind the main cabin. He was cross-legged, but he must have tight hips because his knees pointed sharply up. His hands rested on his knees, palm up. His eyes were closed.

He had no shirt on.

His skin held a light shine of perspiration in the late-afternoon heat. Of course, he had ridiculous muscles—a professional athlete's muscles. She was doomed to see his muscles at some point in the next two and a half days. She only wished it wasn't now. Her nervous excitement and pounding heart ratcheted up three more notches.

Rachel wasn't a meditator. But she knew enough about it to guess that meditators likely didn't appreciate an audience. She would walk away.

Walk away. Walk away now.

His breaths were very long. She saw his lengthy inhale fill his belly, then his chest. His body stilled for a fraction of a second before his lengthy exhale emptied from his chest, then his belly. Then his body went quiet for another fraction of a second.

He repeated the pattern over and over. Inhale, hold, exhale, hold.

It was strange, but watching Evan calmed Rachel's nervous adrenaline rush. She realized she had begun to breathe with him: long inhale, hold a moment, long exhale, hold a moment.

Her body moved in sync with his without touching him. Without him seeing her.

She was careful not to make a whisper of a sound. Their shared breath was a magic spell, and she was afraid to break it.

Her heart beat steadily now. Her thoughts came slower and lingered a bit longer before giving in to the next thought. Her jaw, her shoulders, her hands had relaxed and gone slack.

How long had he been sitting here before she came along? Who taught him to meditate this way, on the repetitive wave of the breath? Had he meditated before soccer matches, or was this something he learned later, after being skewered in the press and subsequently leaving his country?

This side of Evan Hughes wouldn't be in a celebrity gossip fishwrap. This was an intriguing and fascinating layer to discover and peel away.

Not that she would be peeling anything else off Evan anytime soon. He wasn't for her, now or ever.

But—she breathed in, held it, breathed out, held it. This was—

Nearby conversation distracted her. She didn't have time to step away before Evan opened his eyes, turned his head, and looked right at her.

This would be lovely to explain. How did you tell someone you didn't mean to bother them, but you wanted to breathe with them because it was so peaceful and relaxing and calming?

There was no way. So she held up a hand and gave a

lame little wave. "Hey."

He seemed about to ask her a question, but something changed his mind. "Hey."

"I was just—" she started. "I mean, we're all supposed to meet here at—now."

"Very good." He slid off the rock and grabbed his new red sponsor shirt off the grass. He slithered into it as Rachel momentarily looked away. Then he picked up a backpack similar to, if pricier than, hers.

The others arrived, mostly in groups of three or four, though there were a few lone racers. The expressions varied: nervous, excited, wary. Rachel tried to arrange her facial features into neutrality. She joined two women stretching on the grass. The woman sitting in a straddle, reaching down the middle, said, "Hi, Rachel," with a smile.

"Hi, um…"

"Dora," she said. "This is Alexa."

Rachel nodded hi to the other woman. Both of them were young, mid-twenties maybe. Dora had a thick braid wrapped around her head. Alexa sported a pair of sneakers that didn't have a day of dirt on them. "Want me to braid your hair?" Dora asked.

"What? Oh—yes. Sure. Thanks," Rachel said.

"Sit here," Dora indicated. Rachel sat cross-legged in the center of her straddle. Dora pulled the elastics out of Rachel's ponytail, which Rachel had placed an inch apart to secure the ponytail's flare. Rachel didn't know how to braid her own hair, though it was the best style to go with when obstacles like barbed wire could catch hair.

Dora's hands moved quickly and confidently through the strands, separating into sections. "That reporter was such a jerk to you earlier," she said.

"Ugh," Alexa concurred. "Such a jerk."

"Like, who would care even if you were seventy-eight years old? You're a total badass."

"It's because you're a woman," Alexa added. "I didn't hear them ask any of the men if age was a disadvantage.

There are definitely some guys here who are legit old."

"Dusty," Dora agreed.

"That Evan Hughes is super-hot, but we're rooting for you all the way."

"Me?" Rachel asked. "You're running, too."

They both laughed. "We're not going to win," Dora said, pausing mid-braid to tuck a stray strand underneath it. "We only entered this thing to see how far we can go. We've run some small obstacle races, a few 5Ks and 10Ks. But we thought a weekend challenge would be fun."

"We'll tap out when we can't take it anymore and need a beer," Alexa added.

"Don't be so quick to tap out," Rachel said. "Don't do it when it's uncomfortable. Push through the discomfort and I think you'll be surprised. We all have more in us than we think."

Dora's hands paused again. "That's true for life, isn't it?"

Rachel nodded but realized she shouldn't until Dora was done. Dora secured the braid with two elastics. "I hope it's not too tight, but I want it to last you most of the weekend if not the whole weekend," she said. "If we need to swim at any point, you won't have wet hair whipping around your head. The braid will hold."

Rachel put her hand up to feel where the braid began at the crown of her head and descended her skull, ending near her mid back. "Thank you. I appreciate this."

"Girls need to stick together," Alexa said. "It would be great to see you beat Hughes. They're already making such a big deal out of it."

"Who is?" Rachel asked.

"I saw it on SPTS-TV like an hour ago. They didn't show any of the press conference, but they were all, 'Britain's former soccer star Evan Hughes tries to make a comeback, but many experts say schoolteacher Rachel Bowen is his best shot at defeat.'"

Rachel's breath caught. She was already on TV? She'd been worried this story would be a filler on the late-night local sports news, not color commentary at lunchtime on a national sports station.

Dora snorted. "First of all, what 'experts'? This race doesn't get coverage, ever. They're only interested in Hughes, and now the woman who might destroy him. He's in retirement, a has-been."

"Washed up," Alexa confirmed.

Well, that cemented it. No one in the obstacle race community would take Rachel seriously after this weekend—they'd think she was pulling a stunt. Except maybe if she won. No one could say anything bad about that, could they?

Pile on another reason she absolutely had to win this race. The prize money for the kids—and to salvage her athletic reputation. She wished she'd never heard of The Golden Crucible, and this wasn't the best way to start her run.

Justin and his entourage had arrived a moment ago, and a hush fell over the crowd. Alexa squeezed Rachel's shoulder at the same time Dora gave her a fist bump with a parting sentiment. "Kill it, sister."

They moved away from Rachel, who turned her attention to the man who'd essentially be their god for the next two and a half days. He would raise the stakes. He would decide what they ate, and when, and if they did. He would dispatch help for the suffering, and he would end the quests of those who fell short.

"I hope everyone is ready," Justin said, exactly the kind of thing Rachel said to a roomful of tenth-graders when she was about to hit them with a pop trigonometry quiz. "We will be monitoring all of you at all times. If your cuff malfunctions, we will go to where we last spotted you and follow the trail until we catch up. If you show no movement for more than six hours, we will assume you are asleep or hurt and we will come to get you. If you're hurt, though, remember to hit the emergency button on your cuff, knowing full well that means you're out of the race even if we bandage you up good. Go be heroes. Dig deep and throw all you have into this. But if you run into trouble, don't be stupid. Got it?"

Everyone nodded.

"This is the last call for you to back out. Right now. You'll have to do it in front of everyone, but if you feel you have to, no one will say a thing. You'll forfeit your entry fee and take an Uber home. Because I don't mind telling you, this race will absolutely suck. Anyone?"

A crow cried angrily in the branches above them. But no human said a word.

Evan felt good. He felt good surrounded by these brave, ballsy people. Some were strong athletes. Some only wanted to see how far they could be pushed before they broke. Every one of them was worthy at that moment, that moment when they could have walked away but decided to press forward.

Maybe they were rivals, but at this moment of shared determination, they were a team.

He caught Rachel's eye and smiled at her. She half smiled back. He liked to think she felt the same thing about them all being a big team. But it was more likely she was thinking about kicking his ass into next week.

"The trail is clearly marked," Justin said. "I have people in trucks patrolling the length of the course at all times. And I have people manning all the obstacles to thwart any cheating or bypassing. Don't try to do this without sleeping at some point. You won't make it. That's the only tip I'll give you. Every dummy in the past who tried to get through The Golden Crucible without sleeping ended up hurt or collapsed. Not one of them finished. Do you understand what I'm saying? Pace yourselves."

Evan didn't know how much sleep he'd get between the adrenaline and the likely frigid mountain night temperatures, but he agreed. Sleep was crucial and he would do everything he could to get some, even if it was only a few hours at a time.

"By the way," Justin added. "The press are interested in this race for the first time in forever. But they don't get access until the end. I don't want any of those useless idiots tripping, falling, skulking around, and putting you in danger. I told them to wait at the end. The few of you who are lucky to make it to the last thousand feet of The Golden Crucible, wave and smile big so I get some publicity. If none of you make it that far, I guess they'll go home without pictures."

Evan loved the way Justin pretended to not care that his race had made the sports headlines. He had to keep his hard exterior but Evan was sure the race creator was giddy about how many people would sign up for the next race. Especially if someone won on Sunday.

"I don't have anything left to say. It's all you now," Justin said. "Line up."

The runners crowded toward a small rickety sign that read "START" and Evan was sure a seven-year-old had crayoned it. Hardly the pomp and circumstance worthy of a roomful of cameras.

Evan saw Rachel in the middle of the pack, and he moved to get closer to her. But two men in front of her opened up a space and ushered her through, and a few more men did that until she was in the front of the pack. They slapped her back and high-fived her and wished her luck. Then most of them looked back at Evan and gave him thumbs-ups and acknowledgment nods. Evan was proud again to be in this group. In a minute it would be every racer for him—and her—self.

Justin's entourage counted down: "Five! Four! Three!"

Evan's jaw tightened.

"Two!"

He took a deep breath in.

"GO!"

All camaraderie fell off a cliff as the racers pushed and shoved, bottlenecking the entrance to the woods. "MOVE!" the race workers were shouting. "Move! Go! Now!"

Evan had run some races in his athletic life, including a marathon. No one had ever screamed at them before to *move*. They were creating a flee-from-fire urgency that was manifesting a bit of panic among the runners. He saw Rachel break free and sprint off. After another few people squeezed through, Evan took off in pursuit.

It was a rocky trail with an immediate steep uphill reminiscent of the hill that led to the cabins. Evan's sneakers navigated the pebbles well, but he had to keep an eye on the ground to avoid taking a nose dive over a stray rock. He was a fast runner, used to dodging and weaving, usually dodging and weaving players actively trying to block his path. After a few minutes, he hit a stride. He was able to pass a few runners before the trail leveled out. Then he saw Rachel's chestnut braid bouncing in front of him. He caught up to her and ran with her. She was running at a fast but comfortable pace, and they both opened a lead from the pack. He saw her look over her shoulder and assess before she settled back into her pace. Then she turned and looked at Evan for a little longer than he'd have expected her to, considering the treacherous terrain.

"You know," she said conversationally, "the view is much better behind me."

CHAPTER 6

Evan let out a short bark of laughter. "You think you can so easily distract me?"

He tripped over a tree root and swore. She made a noncommittal sound.

"Wow," he said. "Didn't peg you for someone who felt like she needed to play dirty."

"*Need* is a strong word," she said. "And probably an inaccurate one."

They ran in silence for what Evan estimated to be about a mile. Still uphill, but it was a gradual incline now. Two racers ran about five yards ahead of them, but Rachel didn't seem concerned. Evan wasn't. It was good enough to be at the front end of the pack right now, but they didn't need to set the pace. Good to tuck in behind the leaders and follow.

"What's your story?" he asked her after another half mile or so.

"My story?"

"Yes. Where do your parents live? Do you have siblings? Are they athletes?"

"What's your strategy here?" she asked. "Run with me and wear me down with interrogation?"

"Just making friendly conversation. Since we're running

together."

"Why are we doing that again?"

Because I don't want to let you get too far from me in either direction. And I don't want to pause to wonder why. I just don't.

"I don't know why you're running with me," he said. "Probably has to do with my sparkling wit and charming personality. But I'm running with you because I figure you're an expert. You'll know how to conserve energy, and I want to emulate you. I'd be an idiot if I did the opposite of what you did while trying to beat you."

"I'm not an expert. I've never run The Golden Crucible. I've run four—no, five—marathons. And I've run all those OCRs."

"So, no, not nearly an expert," Evan said, letting the words drip sarcasm like honey.

"I'm more of a fan of the shorter obstacle races. I like the challenge of not only running, but running and jumping and climbing and splashing. It breaks up the run. The mental game of a marathon is something I struggled with. And I didn't exactly win, not even close."

"Still, it takes an elite athlete to participate."

"Maybe you could argue that, but that doesn't mean my strategy for this race is sound."

"Your strategy to take each obstacle as it comes, study it, make a plan, make a plan B, and take your time executing?"

They ran in silence for a few minutes. "I didn't know who you were when I gave you that tip."

"I'm glad you did. I didn't have to weasel it out of you. You were happy to offer it when you thought I was a helpless sap."

"I don't know if I thought you were helpless. I just wasn't thinking about you being serious competition."

They rounded a corner. Evan was nearly decapitated by a slingshot of a tree branch still shivering from the runners in front of them. Rachel easily ducked it. "Pays to be short, I bet," he said.

"For some things," she said. "For others, not so much. I've been in races where the monkey bars are spaced so far apart, you'd think they created them for actual knuckle-dragging monkeys. I've almost had to get enough momentum to jump to each one instead of reaching. It's ridiculous. Those course designers must think women—and small men—are not a factor."

Evan was preparing a sympathetic reply in his head when the path they were on suddenly dropped steeply. He grabbed a narrow tree trunk to step down, and another tree to step down again. He glanced at Rachel, but she was navigating it well. He looked ahead to a manned checkpoint with a course volunteer standing beside a waist-high bin. He saw the runners in front of them moving on.

"What's this?" he asked. Rachel didn't answer. They slowed to a stop at the checkpoint and the volunteer smiled.

"You already started the race," she said. "Now it's time to start The Golden Crucible. Please lift three plates from the bin. You lift two, not three," she added to Rachel.

Evan pulled one out and held it in his hand, feeling its weight. "Five and a half kilograms?"

The volunteer shrugged. "I have no idea about kilograms, but I like your accent. It's fifteen pounds."

Just under seven kilograms a plate. Three of them. Maybe not too terrible. He pulled them out, and the volunteer told them to stash them in their packs. Evan knelt on the dirt. He unzipped his bag, shoved clothing and snacks out of the way, and placed the weights at the bottom. He positioned a soft shirt so it would be between the hard weights and his back. He saw Rachel unzip side pockets and place one weight on either side. He didn't know if that was the better way to do it, but she was working with two weights, not three, so he'd have to carry something in the center anyhow.

Two more men arrived at the checkpoint about thirty seconds apart. The volunteer repeated the instructions for them.

"How far do we have to carry these?" Evan asked her. She shrugged a second time, and Evan couldn't tell if her shrug meant she didn't know or she didn't care to share.

He and Rachel zipped up, secured their packs, thanked the volunteer—for what, though, Evan was unsure—and ran on.

"Thirty pounds," Rachel said. "I don't mind saying this sucks."

"Sucks more for me," he said. "I have forty-five."

"I could have carried forty-five."

"I don't doubt it," Evan said, "but I'd trade places in a second without feeling a bit bad about it, so take the advantage. Anyway, it isn't an advantage. You're what, like ... wait, I have to use American measurement ... a hundred pounds?"

She laughed. "No, about one thirty."

"Okay, so now you're carrying an extra just under a quarter of your body weight. I'm ... about one hundred and eighty pounds, so my weight is a quarter of my body weight."

"That was some very impressive math in your head," Rachel said. "I'm a math teacher, so I would know."

"My point is that you know full well that we are carrying equal weight even if we aren't. As it worked out, we are evenly matched. You weren't given a break on this."

"Fair enough," Rachel said, her voice breathier than it had been earlier.

It wasn't unreasonable to carry forty-five pounds. It was unreasonable to carry it while running an undetermined distance. Or maybe they'd have to carry it all weekend. Who knew?

Rachel hit her foot on a rock, and Evan reached for her elbow to steady her. "I got it," she murmured, but he knew the weight was throwing her off as much as it was him. He worked on adjusting his usual stride to one that accommodated the weight.

They ran in silence for another mile, slowing only to

hoist themselves over hurdles, barrels, and fallen tree trunks, all under the watchful eyes of volunteers. The trail was well marked with caution tape and arrow signs.

"Thirty pounds isn't that heavy," Rachel said on a long stretch of dirt shaded to dusk-like darkness under a canopy of trees even though it wasn't quite dusk yet. "But the longer you carry it, the heavier it feels."

"I'd call this a metaphor for life."

"Hm," Rachel grunted. Just when he thought she'd dismissed his comment, she added, "Someone said something very similar to me before the race. Things that are universally true for racing are true for life."

"Right? You're going along fine, business as usual, then something happens and you're living with the weight of it day in and day out."

"Or you've been always carrying a weight, and after several years, it starts to feel heavier and heavier."

"Yes." Evan didn't ask more, though he hoped she would share more.

After a while, she did. "You know, I see this with my students often. It's a low-income neighborhood. I see bright kids staggering under the weight of their families' finances. Some students have to work after school and then their grades drop because they're missing homework assignments and not getting enough sleep. And it turns into a weight for me too, to have to see it happen year after year, kids not getting the resources they need in school or out, and missing college opportunities because of it. It's frustrating. It feels heavier than this feels right now."

Another checkpoint in the distance. Evan checked in with his physical well-being. They'd been going less than an hour, and he was a little damp with sweat and definitely getting damper as the metal plates felt heavier with each step. He didn't want to take his shirt off as the backpack would chafe the skin on his back. "Did you have financial issues yourself growing up?" he asked. "If you don't mind me asking. Sometimes we see things that mirror what we went through and that feels awful."

"Our basic needs were met," Rachel said carefully. "It was just my dad raising us. My mom died when I was too little to form any lasting memories of her."

"I'm so sorry."

"Don't be. My dad raised me and my three brothers, two older than me, one younger."

"No wonder you run around like a little ruffian," Evan said. "You played rough with brothers your whole life."

She smiled, then it faded. "I didn't lack for too much, until…"

She stopped, and Evan prodded. "Until?"

"Until I got into Harvard. I got a partial scholarship and financial aid, but it wasn't quite enough. We appealed, but it didn't help. My dad could only afford a state school, where I earned a free ride. He tried," she said quickly. "He did, and when he told me we couldn't do it, I saw that it was eating him up inside, but there were four of us, and—"

"I understand," he said. "And I understand that's why seeing your students struggle is … personal."

"Yes," she said quietly. "It is."

"Do you think you would have done something different?" he asked. "If you'd gone to an elite college?"

"I don't know," she said. "I ended up loving my college, but it might have been nice to have had more options and opportunities to choose from."

They slowed down as a huge monkey-bars rig came into view. Not only monkey bars, though. A series of bars, then a series of plastic balls on ropes to grab onto, and after that, a huge, thick, frayed rope, maybe twelve feet high, at the far end.

The rig was wide enough that four people could move through at a time. Two men were already on the rig, but they looked labored. It wasn't an easy challenge but should they look that exhausted? Maybe their backpacks were too much?

Rachel didn't wait for instructions. She hopped up on

the step and leaped for the first bar. She hung there by one hand, swung gently for a moment—likely trying to catch the different-feeling momentum with an extra thirty pounds on her—before reaching for the next.

Evan jumped to the first bar without the step for assistance. He hung by two hands for a moment, getting his bearings. Then he swung, bar to bar, arms long, rhythmically swaying his body to assist. When he reached for the first ball, he nearly slipped and had to jump onto it and hold it with both hands, instinctively bending his knees into his chest. He cursed to himself, steadied, and moved from ball to ball. It seemed endless, but he was able to slide off the last ball and grab the rope. He maneuvered the rope in a figure four between his feet so with each inchworm up, he could keep hold. He hit the top and carefully worked his way down. Then he turned to see if Rachel had run off. But she was way behind him.

How? She had started before him and he'd seen her monkey-bar prowess.

One of the volunteers standing near him made a loop with his hand. "Again," he said.

"Do it again?" Evan asked. "Twice through?"

"Nah." The volunteer laughed. "Ten times through. Move!"

"Ten times through without falling once?" Evan asked. "You've got to be kidding me, mate."

"You can fall once," the volunteer said, his eyes on Rachel's progress. "You can fall twice. But fall three times, and you're out of the race."

Evan sighed and jogged back to the start of the rig.

***

A nightmare. Evan had made it through eight times, falling once so far. He didn't know what was harder, getting through this stupid crap ten times without landing his ass in the dirt or keeping his watchful eye off Rachel. He told himself he was keeping an eye on her because she was his nemesis and it would help to know how she was doing. He had to tell himself that a few times to drown out the other voice inside him taunting him that he was watching her for other reasons, reasons that decidedly would *not* help him beat her.

In the time they'd been there, the two racers who were ahead of them had passed—though not easily—and had run on a few minutes ago. Two more racers had approached and now were halfway through their laps. One racer fell for the third time, and a volunteer said, "You! Out!"

"That wasn't even a fall! I slipped but I stayed on!"

"Your foot hit the ground and bore weight," the volunteer said. "You're done."

The racer, a young man maybe in his late twenties and built like a linebacker, exploded with anger, yelling and cursing at the volunteers and their unfairness. It was hard to tune him out. Evan saw Rachel fall, her concentration broken. She glared at the outraged racer and jumped back on. Evan was pretty sure that was her first fall, though. He tried to ignore the commotion, even when a golf cart arrived and the eliminated man flipped out more.

Another racer finally said, "Come on. It was fair and you're out. You're ruining it for the rest of us."

He kept cursing but got in the cart and was shuttled off the course.

Evan understood. Not many runners here considered themselves serious winning material, but they all wanted to get as far as possible, not be eliminated two hours in. They had sacrificed entry fees, travel costs, a full weekend, and who knew how many hours of training before they arrived. Everyone who didn't finish would have to explain why to friends and family. It was unfortunate.

The football pitch had been the same way. The players put everything out there, and when things didn't go their way, even small things, they got hot. Evan included.

Halfway through the bars on his last lap, he saw a swish

of red-brown hair rush ahead into the woods. Damn it. Evan tried to make measured moves from bar to bar, ball to ball, and up the rope, but he was distracted by what it would take to catch up with Rachel, and if he had to. She'd be stopped at whatever the next obstacle was anyway. He didn't need to stay with her. Now that he was getting a sense of what The Golden Crucible was throwing at them, it would be better to keep his pace even and consistent and not expend extra energy this early on. He could get by on a little less sleep tonight if necessary.

But after his last rope descent, he picked up his speed as he followed the arrow onto the trail. His thoughts raced along as fast as his legs.

There was no denying that he wanted to get close to Rachel. But he couldn't, for a ton of reasons. First, he wasn't sure she wanted to get close to him. Her demeanor wasn't particularly warm. But she had watched him while he meditated. He was sure of it. Meditation put his senses on hyperalert. He was aware of every sound, smell, and moment because he was present, and he'd been sure she'd stood there for a while. He'd felt her.

Evan's sneaker hit a huge gnarled tree root and he stumbled. *Crap.* He put out a hand to touch the earth but was somehow able to stay upright, and he kept running.

Second: He had to beat Rachel. He'd been planning this public comeback for quite some time, and he had to put it all out there now to win. Winning a difficult physical event like this one would cement himself in public opinion as an athlete again, instead of a retired athlete. It would be easier to get a job as a TV sports analyst if he was considered relevant, especially as he'd been out of the public eye for a couple of years. He couldn't let his attraction to Rachel distract him from what would already be an unpleasant experience of defeating and disappointing her.

And third, Rachel would absolutely not love being a public-figure girlfriend. He was certain of this because even his ex-girlfriend had not loved it despite being a public figure herself, more so than him. Plus, Evan didn't trust himself anymore after all that. He hadn't expected to turn out to be one of those "non-commitment guys," but he was and he wouldn't waste another woman's time.

Bottom line, he had a goal, and Rachel was the goalkeeper. And he was good at getting past those.

The woods were getting dark, and it was probably time to pull out his headlamp. When he saw a figure crouched on the ground about fifty yards away, he ran toward it to find Rachel tying her sneaker. She already had her headlamp on and shining.

"Fancy meeting you here," he said.

"You've got to get better at the lines," Rachel said. "Cliché city."

"Give me a break. I'm preoccupied. I'm pretty sure three of my vertebrae have broken off under this weight and are floating around in my body somewhere."

She chuckled.

"I know you don't like me," he said, "but maybe you could not laugh at my dire injury."

"I'm not laughing at your made-up injury," she said. "Or I am, kind of. It made me think of the board game *Operation*. Remember that? You had to use little tweezers to pull plastic bones out of this poor guy's body, and if you accidentally touched anything else, it went *bzzzt!*"

Evan lifted his brows, amused.

"I was just imagining," Rachel clarified, "a group of surgeons all gathered around you, trying to find your floating backbones, and having carefully to pull them out." She laughed, and so did he, but mostly because her laugh was so amazing. He hadn't heard it up until now, or seen it, and hadn't known how she laughed from deep in her throat with her mouth open. It filled him with joy.

"Sorry," she said. "It wasn't that funny. I just feel like I need a laugh after the stress of watching that guy back there lose it."

"Can't blame him, really," Evan said, sliding his pack off

his back and rooting through the front pocket for his headlamp. He fished it out and secured it around his head.

"No," Rachel agreed. "I would have been angry too, but at myself."

"He was definitely angry at himself. He had to curse everyone else there to save face."

She nodded, and he flicked his light on, angling it up so he wouldn't blind her. She smiled again. "You look like a real nerd with that."

"I can handle looking like a nerd," he said. "Although I don't know why you think you look better in yours."

"I'm sure I don't. But I can't see me. I can only see you."

"Well, I can see you fine, and you look—" Evan cut himself off. Not a time to start something with her. That appropriate time would be never. "Let's go," he said, pulling his pack back on. "Think anyone would notice if I tossed these metal plates into the woods?"

"Uh, yeah."

"You're right." He ran, and she eased into his pace.

"Seems like a lot of people are getting delayed at the monkey bars/rope thing," Evan said after a while. "It's kind of quiet behind us right now."

"Why did you say I don't like you?"

He didn't answer for a few minutes. "There's no compelling reason for you to like me."

"Why would you say that?"

"I'm sorry. I shouldn't have said it."

"I mean why would you think that to say it?" Rachel asked.

"Well," he began, "I vastly underestimated you the night we met."

"Most guys would have."

"I told you, I'm not most guys. I was disappointed in myself. On top of that, my presence in this race has gotten some attention. That seemed to throw everyone for a loop, most of all you, since you got some nasty questions and an outfit that looked small enough for a five-year-old to wear.

You look good in it, by the way," he said, cutting her a side glance. "On top of that, I fully intend to beat you and squash whatever plan you have for the prize money, and I think you know I have a good shot. So yeah, there's no reason at all for you to like me."

"It's not..." Rachel trailed off. "It's not personal."

"So if I wasn't your biggest rival in this race, you'd be my best friend right now?"

"Well, no," she said. "But that's because it's a distraction. The last time I had a boyfriend, for about eight months—a few years ago—I won nothing. Literally no races. And I raced plenty that year. I hit no PRs. I met very few goals. I was always preoccupied with something having to do with him or with us, usually stuck playing a game with him where we tried to outdo each other. Pretty much like all men I've bothered with in my life. My concentration was shot. My focus was divided. It wasn't a good combo."

"When you said I'd be a distraction, I thought you meant like a pesky fly, not like a boyfriend."

"No, I didn't mean—ugh," she said. "Forget it."

"I will not forget it because now I know you're into me and that's distracting for me."

"I am not into you," she said through gritted teeth.

"Right, right. It's not personal at all." This was fun.

"You know what? That pesky-fly analogy is starting to resonate." She picked up her pace and sprinted ahead, but not too far. Even to make a point, she wouldn't be so foolish as to waste her energy for no reason when they didn't know what challenges awaited them around any corner.

Rachel had been right about one thing. The view from behind her was outstanding.

CHAPTER 7

If Rachel wasn't certain it would get her eliminated from the race—and land her at the local sheriff's office—she'd hurl one of her two fifteen-pound plates like a Frisbee at Evan Hughes's smug head.

She sighed. No, she wouldn't. She didn't want to do that. But she did want to lose him.

Ugh, no. She didn't want to do that, either. It helped to have someone keeping pace with you, at least before it became necessary to open a lead. Which she would do, at some point. Just not yet.

And it had nothing to do with the fact that she liked having him around. It would do her no good to deepen their conversations and become friends.

She had a lot on her shoulders that weighed her down more than an extra thirty pounds in her backpack did. She had the secret reason she wanted to win the money. She had her name out there as the woman with the audacity to run against Evan Hughes at her overripe old age. She had pride to protect once the OCR community learned one of their top women was slumming it in this stunt race. With this stupid event and everything around it, and Evan psyching her out, giving in to mental stress wasn't her thing. Her mind game was strong; it always had been.

Suddenly Rachel—the woman who'd run marathons for a decade, who fell in love with obstacle-course racing five years ago and had landed on the podium for nearly every race in the last three years—was at a disadvantage.

Evan should be the one at the disadvantage. He wasn't used to this kind of physical event. He was right to latch on to her side and borrow her strategy.

But if he wasn't in good enough shape, he wouldn't be able to synergize with her if he'd wanted to. She should have known looking at his bare torso before the race that he was in good enough shape. And that *good enough* was a laughable term for that kind of specimen of man flesh.

Ugh. Rachel pushed her feet forward. The trail got rockier and she had to keep her eyes on the ground to skip past, hop over, and edge around tiny obstacles that could spell the end of anyone's race. The big challenges presented to the runners were their main focus, but if they didn't pay as much attention to every stride they took, their negligence could finish their race prematurely.

Rachel was having a crisis of focus but a different kind: Evan took up too much space in her head right now. His flirting would have been fun if it wasn't coming from a place of trying to knock her off her game. He clearly had a reason to need to win, to want to win, to leave her in the dust, to play as physical and as dirty as he had played soccer. But he seemed genuine in his effort to be her friend, or more—in his effort to flirt with her. If they weren't on a race course with so much at stake for her, she'd want to get closer to him.

She would. She might as well admit that to herself because ignoring it only caused dissonance in her brain. But Evan Hughes wasn't a guy to get close to, and not just because the tabloids had dubbed him the worst boyfriend ever, a horrible creature to dare to break Grace Regan's heart—and that was only the headlines. Rachel had no idea what the actual story was and though every story had two sides, she had no way of discerning which story to believe. Not that Evan would tell her, anyway. It was none of her business. But if you were interested in a guy and the Internet boasted six months' worth of tabloid stories about his role in a messy breakup, that was about as red-flaggy as it could get.

Why was she thinking about this? Ugh, losing focus again.

"Stop!"

She halted so fast, she stumbled to one knee. "Ow. What the hell? Evan?"

"Do not move," a voice commanded. A chill came over Rachel.

"I'm here," Evan called. "I'm right behind you."

The first deep booming voice wasn't Evan's, but she'd known it wasn't. She remained completely still.

"In front of you," the dark voice intoned, "is a field of barbed wire. You will drop low and belly crawl through the field."

"How far is it?" Rachel asked.

"Silence."

She shut her mouth, not wanting to.

"You will turn off your headlamp. You too," he called.

"Turn off the headlamp in a field of barbed wire?" Evan asked. "Are you kidding? It's nearly completely dark."

"Turn it off," the voice insisted. Rachel did.

When she did, she saw the field of wire laid out in front of her with pink lights twinkling all over it. It would have been pretty if it wasn't a field of potential eye-gouging. She also couldn't see the end of it, so who knew how long this was going to last?

"Move," the voice said.

"You know," Rachel called, lowering herself to her belly to begin an army crawl. "Not cool to scare a woman by popping out of nowhere and instructing her to not move. Maybe you can get away with that tactic with a bunch of guys, but when you put a woman in this situation she will immediately think she's about to be assaulted. Just a tip."

"Uh, okay," the voice said, its deep timbre wavering. "Very sorry, um, ma'am. Now, if it's okay ... please move."

Rachel rolled her eyes and moved forward on her elbows. She was grateful for the braid in her hair, keeping it close to her scalp and minimizing the chances of her snagging on anything. She edged forward to the first row of sparkling pink lights and ducked under, staying low. She'd try not to lift her head. If she had to look at what was above her, she'd roll onto her back.

"You told that guy," Evan grunted behind her, closer than she'd realized. "He sounded regretful."

"He probably didn't realize how women could interpret his actions," Rachel said, moving along, trying not to stop. Sharp rocks poked into her forearms and elbows. "*And* some men, frankly. This isn't a haunted house and there was no reason for the scare."

"Were you scared?"

Yes. Women were taught to be afraid of the dark, afraid of men in the dark, and for good reason. Rachel had been verbally assaulted several times over the years while out running alone. She'd had to learn self-defense techniques to enjoy her sport on her own time. Yes, she *had* been scared back there, if for a moment. She didn't want to confess the weakness to Evan, though.

"He scared the crap out of me," Evan said, "to be perfectly honest. I never expected that."

Rachel kept moving slowly. This wasn't an obstacle to rush through. It was hard to estimate how far they'd gone from down here. After some time, she was willing to believe they'd gone at least a half-mile or more.

"This," she heard Evan say, "is really unpleasant."

Of all the adjectives he could have used, *unpleasant* was so understated, so funny, and so, like, English, that Rachel couldn't help giggling. The giggles overtook her and she had to stop moving for a minute to control it. Until she felt something bang into her foot. "Wha—"

"Ow!" Evan yelled.

"What happened?"

"You kicked me in the face."

"I didn't kick you. I wasn't moving."

"What do you mean, you weren't moving?"

"I was laughing at what you'd said and I stopped moving to laugh."

"Are you saying you didn't kick me, but that I instead ran my face into your foot?"

Rachel tried not to snort out a laugh but she did. "Didn't you realize how close to me you were?" she asked.

"I guess not. I can see the lights on the wire, and I can see your outline, but your foot blended with the ground so I didn't see it."

She heard him pause. "I think I'm bleeding."

"Did you hurt my sneaker?" she asked. "Did you get blood on it? Because these are my favorite sneakers."

"Well, this is my favorite nose, isn't it?"

She screwed up her face so hard trying not to laugh that it hurt. "I'm moving again, FYI."

"I don't need *that* FYI. The FYI I needed was the one when you stopped moving."

The retort on Rachel's lips fell right back into her throat as her elbows plummeted into several inches of mud. The whole top half of her body collapsed into it, submerging her face for one unpredictable, scary moment. She pulled her face out and called, "Stopping!"

"I heard you splash."

"Mud," she said. "There's mud up here." She moved forward a bit until her whole body fell in. "I'm still on the ground," she informed him, "but I'm in about six inches of mud."

"Okay," he said, a half-second before she heard him splash.

She kept crawling along, watery mud filling her bra, her shorts, her socks, her sneakers. It saturated the bottom half of her braid. Justin had designed this so the repercussions

67

lasted long past the completion of the obstacle. A water challenge right before dark meant being wet as the mountain air temperature plummeted. Luckily she had a little absorbent towel and a change of clothes, but her hair would remain wet, chilling her for a good part of the night.

She was already cold, and it was tough to not be able to see the end of the barbed-wire field. She had no idea how to pace herself without any idea of how far to go. She wanted to move fast to get out of this muddy water, but she risked tiring herself out with a long way to go. She forced herself to keep a steady, not-too-fast pace.

Evan muttered a curse behind her. She was kind of glad for it; she wouldn't have to waste her energy on outward shows of frustration. She could let him do it for her. At least, as long as he stayed with her. Or as long as she let him stay with her.

She squinted, then blew out a breath of relief. She could see the end. The wire field ended one hundred feet ahead. She could see two figures, probably volunteers, silhouetted against what appeared to be lamplight. Rachel tried not to rush but to keep her consistent pace, not trusting that another surprise wasn't imminent right before the end. The ground came up under her eventually and she finished the crawl on dry, dusty earth. It stuck to her wet skin and clothes but she didn't care. She was freezing and happy to be out of the mud.

After clearing the wire, she stood and stretched. The extra thirty pounds on her back had taken their toll, and she was sore in spots she didn't know how to stretch.

"Good job," said the female volunteer. She actually smiled at Rachel. "Your reward." She handed Rachel a cardboard box and a bottle of water. Dinner. "And," she added, "you can drop the weight plates in that bin."

Thank God. As soon as the plates were out of her pack, Rachel felt—well, thirty pounds lighter.

"If you want to take a break to eat," the male volunteer said, "there are picnic tables over there."

Three tables waited, each with a small lamp. Rachel nodded in thanks and watched Evan slither out of the wire field. He looked beyond relieved to shed his forty-five pounds and to receive food. He walked over to Rachel. "Are you stopping to eat?"

"I think I—we—can take fifteen," she said. "Maybe twenty. Did you hear anyone behind you?"

"No," he said. "Though I confess my ears are filled with mud, so I'm not a hundred percent sure what you just asked me."

They headed to the farthest picnic table and set everything down. Rachel rummaged in her pack for her towel and dried herself off the best she could before pulling on a long-sleeve performance tee. She shivered a little but she could change out of her wet sponsor outfit in a while. She was dying to eat.

They pulled out roast beef sandwiches and little cups of salad. The sandwich was generously large and tasted great, despite the muddy grit between her back teeth. She chewed and looked at Evan.

"I'm sorry you bashed your face into my foot," she said.

"I'm sorry you wore appropriate trail footwear with lugs on the bottom."

"Your nose doesn't look broken," Rachel said. "I don't see any blood. You're still your boyishly handsome self."

"Good," he said. "I won't want to look trampled on when they hang my medal around my neck."

"Or when you're looking sadly at me with the medal around my neck, wondering how it all went so wrong."

He snorted and unscrewed the cap off his water bottle. "I'm already asking that."

"What's your story?" Rachel asked him. "Who's your family? You didn't get to tell me earlier."

"You want to know about my family?"

"You know about mine," she said, artistically evading the question.

"Not a lot to tell," he said. "I have two nice parents. My

mom works for a large bank. My father is a college professor. I'm an only child."

"Ah, so all your childhood soccer aspirations were fully indulged?"

"I suppose, but I showed zero athletic promise as a child. I didn't play football with any real interest until I was a teenager, when I was playing a nonserious game with some mates and a teacher remarked I was a fast runner. No one, no adult, had ever gone out of their way before to say I was good at anything in particular, so I took it to heart. I practiced and practiced until I could try out, and I got better from there."

"It's funny to think your talent would have gone hidden if someone hadn't gotten a glance at it and encouraged you."

"You teachers," Evan said, "have more impact than you think you do."

Rachel smiled. "We're not bad."

"I wonder when we're expected to take our long break." Evan crumpled up the foil that had contained his sandwich. "And how, exactly. I didn't plan to haul tent gear with me."

"Me neither. I figure some volunteer along the way will make the suggestion, maybe point us to a safe place. Justin didn't exactly make it clear, did he?"

"No. Did you happen to bring any bear spray?"

Rachel blinked. "Bear spray? Ah, no. None of that."

"Because, you know. Bears."

"Among other things." Rachel ate her last bite and gathered her trash into the box. "I mean, I've been seeing volunteers patrolling the woods as we've been moving along. On foot, and on golf carts. They're discreet but they are around. He must have a hundred people on this course, at least."

"I read in the entry packet that if you volunteer at an event, it's a nice discount on the entry fee if you enter a race the following year. The race changes every year so it's not a competitive advantage to volunteer, but definitely a financial one."

"I also think some of these volunteers are enjoying their duties a little bit too much."

"I know I would," Evan said. "I would be like a prison guard."

"You would not," Rachel countered. "You'd be a big softie."

"If you've ever seen me play football, you'd think differently."

"Well, I did, and——"

"You did?"

Ugh, so, so busted. "Sort of."

"You didn't know who I was this morning."

"Then I did."

"Ah," he said, grabbing her trash and walking it all to the trash cans ten feet away. She watched as he diligently separated the recyclables and deposited it all in the correct cans.

Maybe he'd let that be the end of it. Maybe he wouldn't give her crap.

Nope. "You Googled me," he said, putting his foot up on the bench and rubbing his calf vigorously.

"You would have done the same," she protested. "You would have wanted to know who your competition was and what they were capable of. You would have Googled me if..." She trailed off.

"If I had a laptop? If I knew your last name? If I knew you were an obstacle-course star? If you were standing in the way of my win? I sure would have."

Rachel let a beat go by. "You Googled me?"

"Sure did, superstar, and you are very impressive."

"Thanks," she said. Evan seemed surprised to not hear sarcasm coating the word.

"I'm off," she said. "I want to see how far I get before the next thing happens, break or obstacle or whatever."

He liked how she didn't say, "Let's go," but instead said, "I'm off." She refused to acknowledge that they were legitimately working together here, helping each other at the same time they were benefiting one another with the company. He admired her stubbornness. She adjusted her backpack and broke into an easy post-meal jog across the clearing and back into the woods. He kept pace.

As they ran, he considered how she hadn't brought up what must have come first in a Google search of his name. Maybe she was saving it for some kind of late-race psych-out tactic, but meanness didn't seem to be her M.O. Either way, he might as well address the elephant on the racecourse. "I imagine the tabloids were scintillating reading for you," he said, his voice sounding falsely casual.

"I didn't read those."

He raised a brow, but as they were both running, she wouldn't see it. Instead, he said, "You absolutely did."

"I told you this morning, I don't lie," she said. "And the fact is that I didn't. Did I see the tabloid articles? Yes. Did I see pictures and big screamy headlines? Yes. The UK is even better than the US at that sort of thing, isn't it?"

"It's the worst."

"I got the gist of the headlines. I didn't bother reading the articles."

"Why not?"

"First of all, I was on a recon mission about your athletic abilities. I didn't have time to read steamy details about a love affair gone unfortunate."

"But I—"

"Also," she interrupted, "I literally have no interest in reading one side of a story. You weren't sitting next to me to defend yourself. It wasn't fair. I'm not saying any of those articles weren't true because I wouldn't know. But I am saying it didn't seem right to have all that information about you that you didn't have about me. It isn't—sportsmanlike."

Evan didn't know what to say, so he watched the ground where his headlamp illuminated his steps and said nothing. She had no idea what a generous person she'd revealed herself to be. His friends had read all those articles. Grace's friends. His teammates. His coaches. His fans. Even his parents had read them, though they never discussed anything he didn't bring up himself in conversation. Everyone who knew him, worked with him, spent time with him, or cared about him—everyone had read it, and they treated him differently. Even knowing he had always tried to be a decent sort, they treated him differently. He'd gotten the impression that the people who stood behind him and stayed with him did so despite cracks in their trust caused by the articles.

But Rachel Bowen, whom he'd just met, a woman who had no connection to him besides being his direct competitor, a woman who had every reason to read every column inch of dirt on him that she could find—if not to psych him out with it at some point but to motivate her to beat a bad guy—hadn't read it.

Because she thought it wasn't the right thing to do.

Evan was mystified. He wanted to say something but he had no idea what to say. *Thank you for not wanting to believe the worst of me? Thank you for choosing to see who I am in this race instead of who I am in the public eye? Thank you for showing me some human decency?*

"There's a checkpoint," Rachel said.

They'd only run about two and a half miles since dinner. Evan still felt what he ate sitting in his stomach.

"Hi!" the volunteer said. It was a young woman, maybe twenty-two, with a long blond Viking-girl braid on either side of her head and a perky, oddly genuine smile on her face. "You look like you're ready to rest for the night."

"Is it time?" Evan asked. This woman recognized him. He could tell by the way her eyes lingered on his face. That lingering stare contained something else as well—something he considered her far too young for him for.

"Almost," she said, the bright smile never leaving her face. "You have to get past me, is all."

"Well," Rachel said, "you seem very nice and reasonable. I can't imagine we will have to crawl in mud or carry a bunch of weight, and I don't see any monkey bars."

"Nope! What I have here is much more basic. Should be easy-squeezy for the two of you."

If Evan could have been fooled by this sorority-sister demeanor, the words *easy-squeezy* were a huge waving red flag of foreshadowing. He had a feeling Rachel wasn't fooled either. They waited.

"Okay," the volunteer bubbled. "All you have to do are one hundred burpees, then run down to that sign and back." She pointed to a sign about two hundred yards off. "As fast as you can. Oh—and this is so, so easy for you two—you have to do three rounds."

Three rounds. Three hundred burpees. On a full stomach. Full of that generously huge sandwich.

As if reading Evan's mind, the woman added, "If you throw up, you won't fail. Just please throw up over there because it's kind of gross, and I don't want to see. But as long as you finish all three rounds, you can move on, barf or not."

Evan sneaked a glance at Rachel. He'd seen her do easy burpees this morning, but that wasn't right after dinner. It wasn't three hundred with a bunch of sprinting thrown in for good measure.

"I'll be watching. Go!" the woman said.

Evan sighed and dropped to the ground.

CHAPTER 8

He didn't throw up, and neither did Rachel, but the round of burpees and sprinting left Evan in a cold sweat. It didn't help that the temperature had dropped quickly mid-round, but putting on warm layers didn't feel right while covered in sweat and grime.

Four runners had come up behind them and joined them. A few other female volunteers had emerged from the trees like spooky cheerleaders to offer additional encouragement—and to count burpees and rounds. It appeared everyone would finish, but Evan saw at least one runner stumble off the path to dry heave.

If there was a less fun way to end the day, Evan didn't know what it could have been.

"You can do it!"

"You're a third of the way there already!"

"You're doing great!"

The perky volunteers' constant encouragement was the worst part of the whole thing, though Evan had no idea why. He would have preferred to be left alone or to be yelled at by a drill sergeant than have those happy comments tossed his way every few minutes.

Rachel finished a few minutes before he did, but he saw

her place her hands on her thighs, soften her knees slightly, and bend over at the waist, hanging her head. He knew exactly how she felt. At least, physically.

Maybe he knew how she felt beyond the physical, also. He was ashamed of himself for thinking this when he and everyone around them were trying valiantly not to be sick, but it seemed to him that Rachel was attracted to him. Maybe as much as he was attracted to her. Maybe enough to—

Enough to what? Experience tabloid life? Move to the UK? Not likely. She might like him, but he doubted she'd like the life he'd have to offer a woman.

There was also the small matter of his track record in commitments. Not good. Women complained about men like him in romance novels, TV movies, girl-buddy sitcoms, and self-help books: the man who wouldn't commit. That was why he'd broken up with Grace, and that was why she had publicly vilified him.

The worst part about it was that she wasn't wrong. At all.

He was good at thinking about himself, protecting himself, and creating a future for himself. One of the last things Grace had said to him was that one day, he'd *have* to put someone else first, and that he wouldn't know what to do—

He shook his head to clear it. This race was messing with his mind more than his physical well-being. "Are you all right?" he asked Rachel.

"Yup," she said, head down. "I got it."

"Got what?"

"It. I got ... my food still in my stomach. I got ... control. I got it."

"If you say so."

He watched a couple of runners stumble off after finishing, but he didn't have the energy to go after them. He crawled onto the ground and wrapped his arms around his legs. He stayed there for a few minutes until Rachel came

76

closer to him. Then he mumbled into his folded arms, "I want my mum."

Her laugh felt satisfying. At least his self-deprecating humor was intact. "I have a feeling that some kind of rest will be encouraged or suggested up ahead," she said. "Maybe there's an actual place to sleep."

He unfolded himself off the ground. The roiling waves in his stomach had passed and the sweat dried. His skin was cold, though. "What, you think there's some kind of lit, cozy cabin up ahead with a wood stove?" he asked. "I could use that right around now."

"We certainly paid a high enough entry fee to merit that," Rachel said. "But I have to say I highly doubt it. I was thinking maybe there's a place to camp or something. If I don't get into dry clothes"—she looked down at her shivering self—"or, you know, actual clothes, I'll be in trouble."

"You didn't have to wait for me," Evan said.

"Yeah," she answered. "I know."

She studied his face, and he returned her gaze. Mud was caked around the sides of her nose and in her eyelashes. Perspiration clung to her forehead, but her back teeth were chattering just a tiny bit from the drop in air temperature. In the new darkness, he wondered if the red in her hair would gleam under the moonlight.

She was a warrior. She was gorgeous.

He was utterly lost.

He jogged because standing there and looking at Rachel felt—risky. And it had nothing to do with their fellow competitors.

She fell into step beside him. The wind picked up, and so did their pace. Evan wished he had a clue of what could come next. He hoped against hope it was something conciliatory. Surely they'd be rewarded for getting this far.

After about another mile, they reached a checkpoint— this time, a tent on metal poles. A college-aged male volunteer had his arms wrapped around his body, rubbing his arms up and down briskly. Rachel reached the large folding table a few steps before Evan did.

"Tents," the young man said, handing each of them a heavy, awkward bundle. "And everything you need to set them up. Sorry, no space heaters, but a blanket is rolled in each tent for you."

The relief Evan felt was immense. "Thank you so, so much," he said. "Where do we pitch the tents?"

"Honestly," the volunteer said, pushing up his glasses, "you could pitch them anywhere. You can feel free to run another five miles and pitch it there. Or you could put them up ten feet that way. Either is fine. I'm not an athlete, but I'm willing to guess it's not easy to run while carrying these things, so you may want to do it closer rather than further."

"Do we have to bring them back here when we are ready to move on?" Rachel asked.

"Nah, collapse them and leave them and the blankets right on the spot and someone will be coming through to pick them up tomorrow. A few things, though: One, don't pitch in the middle of the path to make sure no one runs into you in the middle of the night. Take it a few feet off the path."

"Clearly," Rachel said.

"But two, don't go more than a few feet off the path because we'll be patrolling all night and we want to be able to see everyone. If you go deep into the woods, you assume a lot of risks. There's plenty out there at night here in New Hampshire that I wouldn't mess around with. Stay near the path, where there will be activity all night."

"Understood," Evan said. But was it really? He was a city boy with a tastefully and expensively decorated flat in London he owned and to which he intended to return. He didn't know what was out in the New England woods, honestly. He had been living with his friend in Rhode Island, but it was a near drive to Providence, a cute and up-and-coming city. He'd trained on trails, even did some after-dark training, but he hadn't camped overnight. It was an unfortunate time to discover the gap in his skills, but here it was. What kind of skills prepared you for bears? And— mountain lions? Or—he didn't want to guess what else. He did know that his sleep tonight would probably be more like an open-eyed rest than an actual six-hour slumber.

That reminded him. "We're only allowed to rest for six hours, mate," he said to the kid. "But they took our phones."

"Right, sorry." The volunteer handed them each a small metal box. Rachel used her fingernail to hit the catch and spring it open to reveal an alarm clock.

"What?" she said. "This is hilarious. My grandmother used to have one of these. Did Justin buy a pile of these on eBay or what?"

The volunteer shrugged and Rachel marveled at the clock for another couple of seconds before snapping it shut. "Thanks," she said.

"Yes, thanks a lot," Evan echoed.

"You're welcome. And good job," the kid added. "Only the first eight people get blankets."

"Really?" Evan asked.

"Yes, and the first thirty-five get tents. The rest of them will be pretty cold."

"If they last the night without quitting," Rachel said, brows lifted. "Do you know if any have dropped out so far?"

"I've been notified that thirteen have dropped out so far."

"Thirteen? Are you kidding?" Evan asked. Already?

"A bunch of people fell three times on the bars. A few people crawled off after the burpee sets. One person had an emergency at home and someone had to come get him. This is actually pretty good," the kid said. "I volunteered for The Golden Crucible competition last year and about twice that many were done before the first night was over. You guys are tough."

"Any hints at what's coming tomorrow?" Evan asked.

"Oh, I couldn't tell you."

"You couldn't?" Rachel asked. "Or ... maybe you really want to tell us?"

"Just a hint," Evan chimed in. "If we can't do it, we can't do it, whether we knew about it or not. So it's not at all cheating."

"I wouldn't be cheating by telling you," the volunteer said. "But you're sort of cheating by asking, aren't you?"

"He's right," Rachel said to Evan. "I shouldn't have asked." She leaned over and put her hand on his arm warmly. "I'm sorry."

The kid looked at Rachel's hand on her arm, then at her face, and said, "Oh, hell, just don't mention I told you. From here it's about a twelve-mile run to the next obstacle. So you basically start off your morning with a very long run. I don't know what you'll find at the end, though."

"Thank you," she said. "I mean that. I'll know what to eat for breakfast from my pack and that will help a tiny bit."

"Have a good night," the volunteer said, pushing up his glasses again. "Be careful."

Evan and Rachel trudged away, each with a cumbersome tent tucked under an arm. "I don't know what the right move is here," Rachel confessed. "Just sack out here and gain ground in the morning, or try to get another mile or two in and have a lead on most of the pack."

"How are you at a twelve-mile morning run?"

"I'll be great," she said. "A long run is what I'm good at. I can cover a lot of ground fast. And I love to run early."

"Then I think your best bet is to make up the time in the morning," Evan advised. "Why waste time gaining slow ground now when you can use that time to rest? Change your clothes, dry off, eat something when you wake up, and get a move on."

Rachel was nodding before he'd finished speaking. "You're right. Thanks. I'm going to move far enough away from the checkpoints though, so I don't hear people talking when they stop there. So I can hear other noises around me to stay safe."

It was strange how they were suddenly talking about themselves as solo racers, instead of the little unexpected alliance they had formed. Evan would have to open a lead at some point, but he had something like thirty-six hours before he had to have a comfortable lead on her and everyone else.

"How many people do you think are in front of us?" he asked.

"I'm sure it's just two, and it isn't a massive lead. I'm not too worried about them opening up yet. A few ambitious people will try to get a jump on us at dawn, but I'll be ready because this part will be my strength."

A nice long run would work fine for Evan too, but he kept it to himself for now. He'd run one marathon and a few half marathons, not easily but with good times. He'd run miles every day since retiring. He might even run more a day now than on match days back then. This part would be his strength too, but he didn't want to announce that yet. She probably suspected as much anyhow.

He also assumed that tomorrow's obstacles would be a nightmare and would make today's look like playground games.

Of course, they mostly were playground games— running and monkey bars and climbing ropes.

"Do you need help with your tent?" he asked.

"Do you?" she retorted.

"Probably," he admitted. "They took my phone so I'm unable to search 'how to pitch a tent' on YouTube. I might be in trouble here."

"You can always lay it flat like a tarp, lie down on one end, hold the edge, and roll yourself in like a burrito."

She was teasing. Evan was pretty sure, at least. But the burrito would probably be a good idea if all else failed.

"It's nice of you to offer," she relented, "but like I said, I have three brothers. I've been pitching tents for camping trips my whole life. I've got this."

She moved off the trail a few feet and laid the tent bundle down. He set up a few yards away. He tried not to watch her as she worked—or rather, he tried not to let her see he was watching her—and he fumbled with his tent until he figured it out. It was actually pretty intuitive, and he got it standing in about fifteen minutes. A little wobbly, but hopefully solid. He rolled his blanket out on the bottom and sat. Not the softest accommodations he'd been offered, but he could lie on one end of the blanket and fold the other half over him. He wondered what kind of bed Rachel had at home—he couldn't imagine a frilly bedspread or dust ruffles. He wouldn't be surprised if he learned she slept in an Army cot with a scratchy burlap blanket, with rough white sheets she tightened to quarter-bouncing perfection every morning.

Of course, he didn't know if she shared her Army cot—or queen-sized bed, or whatever it was—with anyone. Her male-female interactions with him were in no way over the top. And she didn't seem like someone who would be slightly attracted to someone else if she was in a real relationship. She seemed like someone who would be a great girlfriend, just as she was amazing at everything else he'd seen her do so far. Something motivated her—money, yes, she'd said that, but in Evan's experience, this kind of push didn't come from needing or wanting money. This competitiveness came from something else, something in the past, something else that needed to be fulfilled.

Maybe she would share what it was. Or maybe she'd punch him in the nose if he asked. Both seemed equally likely, and it deepened and strengthened his attraction to her even more.

He was a stupid, stupid man.

He undid his backpack and changed hurriedly into dry, warm clothes. A long-sleeve rash guard, a light fleece zip-up and running pants, dry socks. He laid his wet clothes out flat in the small space beside him but was pretty sure it would be too cold for them to dry overnight. He had a change of warm-weather clothes for tomorrow, but who knew how dirty and wet they'd get with whatever gauntlets were thrown down tomorrow? Then he'd have gone through all his clothes with another day to go.

"You look like you did okay," he heard from outside his tent. He pushed aside the flap to find Rachel crouching outside, examining his tent with one eye squinted. "It looks like it will hold up, actually."

"Not bad for a posh footballer," he admitted. He poked his head out and looked at Rachel's tent, which listed drastically to the left. "What's happening to your tent, Miss Campfire?"

She shook her head. "It's broken. One of the poles is all messed up."

"Go get another one."

"They won't give me another one. You heard the guy earlier. We're lucky we got tents. He won't swap one out for me."

"You managed to get him to tell you we're starting with a long run tomorrow morning. What's to say that same charm won't get you a new tent?"

"I feel guilty asking. This was my designated tent, and I'd be taking one away from someone else."

"That's very noble."

"Shut up."

"I wasn't being sarcastic!" Evan protested. "It's admirable. If you have trouble, let me know and I'll see what I can do. Probably nothing, but I promise to try."

"Thanks." She half smiled.

"Well, you're welcome to join me and chat, unless you're going right to sleep."

Rachel hesitated. Evan wondered if the invitation felt too intimate. But she looked over her shoulder, then crawled into the tent.

She had changed her clothes as well, and was now in a bright yellow jacket and long pants. She had taken off her wet sneakers as he had, and she wore thick socks.

"Do you have a torch?" he asked.

"No," she said. "A torch? Is this *Gilligan's Island?*"

"No, sorry. Uh—a flashlight."

"Oh, an English-ism," she said. "I left mine in my tent. I didn't expect to hang around here. But my tent's just a few steps away so I won't need one."

They sat together in silence. Their previous running silences had been comfortable, but this one was awkward. Probably because she sat right where he'd be sleeping.

"It's like a slumber party," he said.

"Yes, like a weird slumber party with boys allowed and no sleeping bags or pizza. But otherwise, sure," she said, laughing.

"It's so dark I can't see the details of your face."

"I know. It's kind of nice."

"Not interested in looking at my face, then?"

"I know what your face looks like. It looks kind of flat from running into my shoe."

"You'll never let me forget that, will you?"

"When your ghostwriter writes your soccer—football—autobiography, send them to me so I can give them some good stuff."

"Will do," he said.

A few more awkward minutes went by. "I heard people setting up nearby," Rachel said. "I don't think many people ran ahead carrying tents."

"I don't think many people made it this far tonight," he pointed out.

"True."

More silence.

"Hey, you want to play Truth or Dare?" he asked.

"Aren't we on a weekend full of dares? I'm not sure I'm willing to add to it."

"Well, how about we just play Truth?"

"That seems like the unfun half of Truth or Dare," she said, "but hey, why not? You go first."

"Go first asking a question or go first answering one?"

"Whatever you want."

"I'm not seeing much of your competitive spirit in this game," he said. "Or is that only where physical challenges are concerned?"

"I'll ask a question. Truth or ... truth?"

"Wow, not an easy choice, but I'll go with truth."

"Okay." She paused. His eyes were now accustomed enough to the dark to see she was looking at him, weighing her options. "Do you think you'll win?"

"I did think that," he said. "But that press conference rattled me a bit. Hearing the race credentials of a couple of those guys, but especially yours, broke my confidence somewhat. I think I'll finish at the front, but whether it's as first remains to be seen. I want to, though. As you know, I want to make a positive athletic comeback, so I can be in the news again, but this time having nothing to do with my personal life."

He saw her small nod in the dark. "My turn," he said. "Truth or truth?"

"Hmm, either one. I'm feeling sassy."

"Got it." He waited a moment. "What's the prize money for?"

She didn't say anything.

"I'm sorry. You don't have to—"

"It's for the kids in my school," she said. "The high school I teach at is in a very low-income neighborhood outside Boston. The kids don't get what a lot of other, richer Boston-area schools get in terms of technology. Or they get them, but they get outdated versions of everything because it was cheaper. Anyway, the school budgeted for and finally got the go-ahead to build out a new lab. The lab was created to be a new technological maker space for students to get hands-on experience and training with things like 3D printing. These students—they are so smart, but they are held back by their circumstances and this way, they can have some real project experience to add to their college transcripts."

"That's amazing. I'm guessing you had a lot to do with the vision of this space."

"Yes, but the entire math and science staff is psyched and contributed ideas and held fundraisers and all kinds of other things. The students were so excited when it was announced. They went crazy. They've all been volunteering and helping out to make the space perfect."

She fell silent, and he prodded gently, "But—"

"But," she echoed. "The community voted down the most recent budget and the school is now on austerity. They have this beautiful, dedicated space but no money for equipment. It's been sitting unused for months."

"You mentioned the school budget when we met. What a shame."

"It is. I had the bright idea that I could maybe get into a race that has some good prize money. I race most weekends when it's not the dead of winter, and I've podiumed often, so I know my sport. I know my likely competitors and I signed up for the Prestige Race. Prize was $10,000 to the winner, and about half of that to the second-place finisher, and a little less than that to third place. I was certain I could get a piece of it, if not outright win. I knew the course ahead of time—unlike this race—and it was an eighteen-miler. Very doable."

"I see another *but* on the horizon. You lost."

"I lost. I don't know if it was because I suddenly had something important riding on a win and I was distracted, or if I hadn't trained enough in the few weeks leading up to it because I was so confident, but I crashed and burned. I came in fourth."

If anyone knew about the disappointment of losing, it was Evan. "You must have been miserable."

"The thing is," she said, "I made the dumb, dumb, *dumb* mistake of telling a couple of my students about it. They actually all know I'm an OCR competitor, and they think it's cool. They often ask me on Monday mornings if I raced and how I did, and a lot of them are friends with me on

Facebook. They see pictures of me with medals and whatever and they are fascinated with it. A few students tried it one summer. It's expensive to enter so I took care of them, and they had a great time. Anyway, I told a few students I was running the Prestige and if I won, I was hoping to get their maker space equipped, and though I asked them not to tell anyone, they're kids, and they told everyone, and I had to badly disappoint them that Monday morning."

She shook her head. "It felt awful. These kids suffer a lot of heartache for all kinds of reasons, at home and elsewhere. I felt like the worst human in the world to hand them another defeat."

"It wasn't your fault," Evan said. "If I know anything, it's that a win is never a sure thing. Surely high school kids are old enough to understand that."

"They understood and not one of them blamed me, of course, but they were so—I just wanted to give them this one."

"And so now you're here for prize money."

"The Prestige Race doesn't happen for another year. The Golden Crucible was the race coming up the soonest with a significant prize. Seventy-five hundred dollars isn't a fortune, but it could buy them good wholesale equipment. These kids don't have time to wait until the voting community realizes that education helps everyone. They have college to think about."

"That's why you are not happy with the press coverage," he said. "That's the real reason why you didn't want anyone to know you're running this race. You said it was because this wasn't a respected race in your circle."

"It isn't, and it's true I'd have preferred if people didn't know. But thanks to you being in this race, they'll find out now if I win. I think at that point, I can explain that I did it for a good educational cause and I don't think I'll get too much grief about it. But yeah," she said, stretching her legs out in front of her and rubbing her hands up and down her calves, "I didn't want to lose and disappoint the kids again. I wanted to run under the radar and give them a happy surprise when I win."

"You're talking again like victory is a sure thing. Even after your last loss."

"That's how I stay focused and positive," she said. "I can't entertain the possibility of defeat. Not before a race. If I lose, I can deal with it my way after the fact. I've talked way too much," she interrupted herself. "Truth or truth?"

"Let's go with truth," Evan said, leaning back on his elbows.

She didn't say anything for a minute. She seemed to be searching his face for permission. "Whatever it is, it's fine," Evan said. "We're playing Truth or Truth. The only rule is to tell the truth. I suppose I could be a wanker and opt out if I want to keep something to myself, but you told me something important and fair is fair."

"Okay," Rachel said. "What do you want to do after this, if you've met your goal of significant-enough interest in you following this athletic endeavor? You said a comeback. What kind of comeback?"

"Not a football one, not directly," he said. "I have no interest in managing or coaching. I'm done with being on the pitch. But I could be happy as a TV analyst, or something else on TV. Or I could have a line of sports gear. Grace had her own line of clothes, and she—" He paused. "She liked it," he finished lamely.

In the shadows, Rachel saw his face darken a bit. "You still care for her?"

"No," he said. "I mean, yes, I care about what happens to her and if she's okay. I just don't love her. Not anymore. I knew I didn't, and that's why I broke it off."

"You don't have to tell me this," Rachel said. "I know it's Truth or Truth, but I wasn't going to ask about that. It's not my business."

"I don't mind," Evan said. "In fact, it feels cathartic to say it. I haven't talked about it in a long time. I feel like this race is tormenting my old body, so I might as well purge my soul as well and get it all out. Win or lose, I'll finish on Sunday a new man."

"If you want to tell me, I'll listen. I won't judge."

"We all judge," he said. "Even when we try not to. Everything we hear and learn is filtered through our perspective. I appreciate you not wanting to judge, but you will, and that's okay."

"That's some pretty big insight into human nature. I'm not sure I signed up for that this weekend."

"Sure, you did. What is this entire event if not insight into human nature? Competition. Man—and woman—against nature. Will power. Confronting the strong desire to give up when things get tough. Which is kind of what I did in that relationship. I gave up. I didn't want to commit. I never thought I was that cliché guy who didn't want to commit, but when the time came and she was hinting at a long-term thing, I couldn't do it. I had to tell her."

"Oh," Rachel said, and she was oddly disappointed. It wasn't like she needed him to be a commitment guy. She didn't need him to be anything. She didn't need him.

"Yeah," he said. "She didn't see it coming. I honestly didn't either, but as soon as I realized it, it was wrong to let her think otherwise and I had to tell her."

"At least you were honest."

"I didn't win any points for honesty," he said. "With her or with the tabloids. The public loves her, and I don't begrudge them that. I do wish she hadn't told them what an awful guy I am, but she wasn't wrong."

"Do you believe that?"

He paused a moment. "I think I do. I'm that jerk who wouldn't commit when the time came. Which is unfortunate, because…"

"Because?" Rachel prodded and immediately wished she hadn't, because you couldn't put all the released enchantment back into Pandora's box.

"Because I feel like there's something going on here."

Rachel had been aware of his closeness since she'd first sat. She was aware she was sitting where he'd lie down to sleep. She was aware they had very little to keep them warm, to keep them safe, to keep them fed. It felt like their lives had been stripped down to the basics. Intimacy was a basic, and it swirled around them both now.

"Unless I'm reading this totally wrong," Evan said. "In which case, I apologize. You might be thinking about your bodybuilding boyfriend right now and I'm way off base."

"I'm not thinking about my bodybuilding boyfriend."

"Ah, so there is one."

"There is not. No boyfriend. An ex-husband long gone, and some boyfriends after that, but no current boyfriend. It's been a few years since I was in anything serious."

"So there's something? Here, I mean."

Rachel's body felt tingly and alive in several private places. She was sure Evan could hear her heart beating; it was almost all she could hear. "You aren't a fan of scandal," she managed to say. "And this is one, if anyone sees me with you in your tent late at night. I need to go back to my own."

"I guess that's your way of letting me know there isn't something."

"Oh, there is," Rachel said. She didn't want to raise her voice, so she lowered it to an insistent whisper. "There's a something. You said it, and I won't bother denying it. But here's what's in the way of that something. I need to beat your butt this weekend, as you know. And as you know, you're not a commitment guy. And also, as you know, your love life is of national interest to your home country, or has been. That's so many red flags waving, I'm surprised a bull doesn't come charging through here."

She shut her mouth, sure she had hurt his feelings. But at some point in her speech, he'd moved closer to her. He reached out and tucked a stray strand of hair behind her ear. His hand hovered near her cheek. She stopped breathing.

His gaze dropped to her lips.

She stood up abruptly, and he leaned away. "Go to

sleep," she said. "This is weakness. This is exhaustion. This is vulnerability. This is *not* what we should be doing."

He nodded, then inclined his head toward the flap of his tent. She ducked out and ran in the cold to her precarious, leaning-Tower-of-Pisa tent.

She crawled in and fastened the flap shut. She wrapped herself in the blanket and lay on the thin floor. She felt every little sharp corner of every rock underneath her body.

She felt the same way right now as she had each time she was able to conquer an obstacle in the race. This was the biggest challenge so far. A man who wanted her, who was hot as hell, funny, strong, and—it seemed to her—very kind, but was everything she didn't need. He stood in the way of giving happiness to her kids. But now she was in her own tent. She had managed to disentangle herself from the spell that had woven its way around her heart and her mouth and her—well, yeah.

She was in the clear. She could race alone. She could stand alone. And she could damn well sleep alone.

Rachel heard a snap, then a creak, then the tent fell onto her head, covering her in a sea of nylon.

CHAPTER 9

"Evan," she whispered as loud as she dared with other tents in hearing distance. "Evan!"

Though she couldn't blame the guy for sleeping like the dead after the day they'd had, she wished he was more of an insomniac. Someone else might hear her and come over to investigate.

She stepped into his tent and closed it up. She kneeled next to him and put a hand on his shoulder. It was warm. "Evan," she whispered again, but this time not as loud. "Wake up."

And wake he did, with a gasp that scared Rachel into gasping too; then she cupped her mouth with both hands so they wouldn't be heard. "I'm so sorry," she whispered.

"What's wrong?" he asked. "Are you okay?"

"My tent fell down," she said and started giggling. How could she not? It was ridiculous. "My tent fell down, and I couldn't sleep in the wreckage."

"Do you need help securing it?"

"The pole snapped in half," she said. "There's no securing it. It's done."

"Do you want to stay here?"

No. Yes. No. "It's cold," she rationalized, "and with

both of us in the tent, we heat it up a little bit."

"You could say that."

"I didn't mean it like that. I just meant—it's practical, and benefits you too, if we share. But we can't talk. I don't want anyone hearing us. And I'll have to be careful in the morning so no one sees me. I don't snore or talk in my sleep, at least as far as I know, and I brought my own blanket."

"Well, letting you freeze into a popsicle overnight would be effective, but it doesn't seem like a fair way to win. How long did it take you to decide to come over here?"

A while. "Just—is it okay?"

"Yes," he said. "I could use an extra blanket and another body for heat."

"I can sleep over there." She gestured vaguely to the other side of the tent.

She moved to as far a corner of the tiny six-foot space as possible, which was only inches away from him. "Good night," she said. "I brought my alarm."

"Mine's set. We won't oversleep. Good night."

Rachel hunkered down on the ground, wrapping the blanket around her. She covered her entire body, even her head, and tried to breathe through her mouth, hoping her own breath would warm up the space inside the blanket wrap.

She heard Evan shift on the ground, then go silent. He wasn't sleeping, though. Tension hung in the air, not sleep. He was holding out for—whatever might happen.

"Hey," she whispered.

"Yes?"

"Please don't tell anyone I slept here."

"I won't. We'll make sure no one sees you in the morning. We'll be careful."

"Thanks."

"It's for me, too," he said. "Like you said, I've had enough scandal to last me forever."

"Right." She closed her eyes. She was exhausted. She shouldn't have to lie here very long before sleep took over, no matter how she felt about Evan Hughes.

But lie there she did, for what felt like an hour, hyperaware of every sound, every movement inside the tent. A black bear could be lumbering around outside the tent right now, searching out snacks, and Rachel wouldn't hear a thing because she was observing Evan's every move with her ears. *He's rolling over. He's pulling the blanket around him closer. He's yawning.*

This tension would hold her back tomorrow, and through the rest of the race. She wouldn't be able to concentrate, to get her mind on what she was supposed to be doing, if she entertained this tension. Maybe it would be better to do something about it. Release the valve on the emotional pressure cooker. Giving in might be the easiest way to let it go.

Right?

She fought the blanket, which had twisted around one of her legs. She pulled and kicked until she was free. For a moment, she wondered if the universe was trying to hold her back, trying to tell her something. Then she remembered she didn't believe in stuff like that.

This might not be a good idea. It was possible this was the absolute worst idea she ever had. But her weary body and mind weren't up to thinking outside the box. Rachel saw one obvious solution and she would take it.

Now.

She scrambled on hands and knees over to Evan, who immediately sat up. "Are you all ri—"

Her lips stopped his from forming any more words.

She pressed her mouth hard, maybe to dissuade him from pulling away, but she needn't have worried. His hand came around the back of her head and the curves fit perfectly. He nudged her lips open with his tongue and a sound caught at the back of her throat. Her arms wound around his shoulders, and his arms wrapped around her lower back. He pulled her into his warm spot on the floor of the tent.

She wished she hadn't put fleecy layers on, so all her skin could drink in all of his. He tasted exactly the way she wanted a man to taste. She threaded her fingers through his short blond hair and tightened her fist full of it. He brought one hand up to her face and she took hold of his wrist. He showed no interest in coming up for air, and Rachel was glad for it. She kissed him until she ran out of ways she knew how to kiss—with her lips, tongue, light nips with her teeth—and she had to start all over again.

When he dragged his mouth off hers, she did make a noise then, but he didn't go far. He buried his face into the spot under her left ear and blazed a hot trail of kisses down her neck. The tent, with zero insulation, suddenly felt like a steam bath. She pulled the neck of his shirt and jacket aside and pressed her lips to where his neck met his shoulder. She didn't let go of the material and his fingers clawed at the back of her pullover jacket.

A cough. Outside.

They jumped apart and widened their eyes at each other. But whoever had coughed passed by their tent. Someone up in the middle of the night to attend to business. Rachel and Evan didn't move a muscle until they were certain the person was gone, returned to their own tent.

Then Rachel took a breath. "Ooookay," she whispered slowly.

"Okay?" he whispered back.

"I think we both needed that."

"Superstar," he said, "I didn't need that. I think that was the last thing either of us needed. But I was lying here wide awake, wanting that."

"Tension release," she explained. "I figured we didn't need the tension for the rest of the weekend, so..." Her words faded as she realized how she sounded. Like she was rationalizing her idea to make out with a hot guy.

"Did that release tension for you?" he asked. "My body could tell you the opposite right now."

She sighed. "No," she said. "Okay. Not cool. Sorry."

"If there's one thing I never want you to apologize for, it's what we just did."

They were still whispering.

"Okay," she said. "I'm going back to my corner."

"Hold on a minute," Evan said. "We created enough heat for a tent twice this size. It seems senseless to go back to shivering."

Rachel raised a brow and held it there for a moment until she realized he likely couldn't see it. "What are you trying to say?"

"Sleep next to me. It's warmer for both of us that way."

"Oh, come on," she said. "Don't pull this lame soap-opera trick. 'I'm so cold!' 'It must be hypothermia. Quick, take off your clothes. Our body heat will save your life.' 'Oh, I couldn't!' 'It's for your own good. You'll die without my manly body all over yours.' 'Okay, but my virginity!' 'I'll be a gentleman, never fear.' Then, he's not a gentleman. But—life saved. Virginity lost forever. And an avalanche happens or something and they get buried under rocks. The end."

"I have so many questions," Evan whispered. "First, how many soap operas do you watch? Second, are you trying to tell me you're a virgin? Because someone who kisses like you—yeah, no. And three, is this a prime location for avalanches? Seriously, is it? Because I have no idea what to do if we are buried under rocks."

"What I'm trying to say is telling me to sleep next to you is so cliché."

"Eating three meals a day and brushing your teeth is cliché, but it's what you do to survive," he said. "Yeah, you'll survive overnight sleeping in the corner by yourself. It's not hypothermia cold. But it's a fact that we will be warmer if we absorb each other's body heat. And we'll sleep better. How are you going to win if you have no sleep?"

"How am *I* going to win?"

"Or how am I? How will we beat those chumps out there"—he jerked a thumb toward the tent flap—"who aren't utilizing the body-heat buddy system? I mean, maybe they are. But probably not. And then we'll have an extra advantage. Also, we can double up one blanket under us to cushion the bed of nails I feel like I'm lying on, and we can use the other one on top of us."

Rachel said nothing.

"Look," he said, "we've already eaten away a good chunk of our allotted six hours debating it. Let's get some sleep."

He held out his hand. Rachel turned, grabbed a corner of her blanket, dragged it over, and put it into his hand. He raised to a crouch, spread her blanket, and sat on it, pulling his on top. "Better already. Come on, now."

She closed her eyes before she crawled beside him. He scooted over so the length of his body ran along the length of hers, but he didn't wrap his arms around her, or move to spoon her, or anything like that. He made it clear he was respecting her space, that this was for practicality only.

Rachel wasn't disappointed. That would be foolish. And silly. And ridiculous.

"I only watched one soap opera growing up," she whispered. "But I watched it for twenty years."

"Long enough to see all characters die in avalanches and get replaced by characters just as likely to camp in geographically treacherous spots?"

"Pretty much, yeah." She took a deep breath and relaxed her muscles on the exhale. "Good night."

"Good night," he said. "And I'll be a gentleman, never fear."

She elbowed him in the ribs.

"Oof," he said.

***

In his luxury flat in London, Evan would wake to the sound of zen chimes. From silence, they would fade in, and after a few minutes, they would reach his ears. A few moments after that, they would reach his mind, and his eyes would open slowly and gently to soft light filtering through the long white gauzy curtains.

In a tent in the woods of New Hampshire, Evan awoke to the sound of a shrill, hammering blast of a bell, smashing through his ears and running down his spinal cord like a live-wire electric shock. He sprang up with zero memory of where he was or when he was or what the last thing he did was. "Shut up, shut up, shut up," he rasped from his parched throat as he searched through his blanket for the offensive rattling clock. He found it a few feet away from his makeshift pallet. When he picked it up, it vibrated so violently that his weak-from-sleep hands dropped it. He picked it up again and pressed every button he could find before it stopped. Then, as if he was in some kind of insane dream, the same alarm blasted from elsewhere in the tent. He located it, turned it off the same haphazard way, and waited for another sound grenade to hit. When it didn't, he sat on the blanket, rubbed his face, and tried to piece together what was happening here.

Two alarms—one was Rachel's. Rachel.

He looked right and left, but he needn't have bothered since it wasn't a big enough space for her to hide in. He poked his head out of the tent and looked around. Then he peeled off his warm clothes and changed into shorts and a tee. Fast.

Rachel had taken off. And who knew how long ago? She could have a five-minute head start, or she could have an hour head start. On twelve miles.

Wait, no. She had a head start, but it couldn't be that long because their six-hour rest was mandated. Their carefully set alarm clocks had woken him up, so she'd probably left in the last ten minutes or so. He knelt and touched the space where she'd slept, and it was still warm.

But the woman was a champ. He knew she was flying now, opening up that ten-minute lead to longer.

Yesterday, he'd have fully expected this. Before he kissed her.

No, before *she* kissed *him*.

She hadn't run ahead. She'd run *away*.

CHAPTER 10

Dressed and sneakered, Evan shoved his belongings into his backpack, except for one protein bar. He tore open the package and ate it without tasting any of it. He stumbled out of the tent, then collapsed it and ran down the path. He saw two runners ahead of him, running at a faster clip than Evan would, not knowing the way he did that they had twelve miles in front of them. Once it dawned on them that this day was starting with a long run, they'd take a break and Evan, who'd be pacing himself, could easily pass them.

Evan didn't know what his goal was anymore. Was it to win? Was it to beat Rachel specifically? Or was it to somehow salvage something he could build upon with her after this race was over? If it was the latter, she made it clear by bolting this morning that wasn't her goal in the least.

Running in the early morning was something Evan usually loved. He knew runners ran listening to music, or a favorite podcast, but he never listened to anything but his own breathing, his own footsteps, his own heart pounds, and his own thoughts. The only soundtrack he needed was made up of morning bird songs, wind rustling the leaves, and the scratch of squirrels' claws as they scampered up tree trunks. Or that was the soundtrack he'd been treated to since staying with his friend in the suburbs of Rhode Island. When he was in London, the early urban morning had a different but oddly soothing sound: buses and cars going by had an ocean-wave quality. Though in London, Evan had tried to run incognito, with a baseball cap or bandanna on his head and sunglasses covering his face. Still, he was recognized at least once a week. If he was lucky, someone just smiled at him or waved to him. If he wasn't lucky, his run was over.

But here, the run was the solitude he loved so much. His thoughts, however, were of one chestnut-haired woman and her determination, strength, and beauty.

And her kiss.

He ran for ten minutes. For nine of those minutes, he thought about her kiss, and he spent the other minute tying his shoelace. But he was stopped at a checkpoint after only that long and given a bucket full of gravel to run with. Evan stopped himself from protesting he was told the night before it would be a twelve-mile run, partly so he wouldn't get that kid in trouble, and also because it was apparent that it *was* a twelve-mile run, just with additional strife piled on. He bear-hugged the bucket, holding one of his wrists with the other, and set out. His run deteriorated into a fast, awkward walk. The path inclined sharply up, and the *fast* dropped off the description. So did *walk*, after a while. Evan staggered. He staggered at a determined pace at least four kilometers of steep uphill. He put the bucket down a few times to stretch and to switch wrists.

At some point, he passed the guys he'd seen ahead of him earlier. They were drinking water and having a snack, their gravel buckets resting on the ground. They waved as Evan passed. There were more than twenty-four hours to go, and, perhaps wisely, no one was trying to make a serious break for it yet. Except Rachel. She could be halfway to California by now, and Evan doubted these guys knew she'd gotten a jump on them this morning.

He wondered if Rachel was given a full bucket of gravel

like he was, or if she'd been given a lighter women's weight. He wondered if being smaller was an advantage or a disadvantage for her, or if it didn't matter. He wondered if she was wondering how he was doing. He liked to think so, and so he continued to think so.

After about another kilometer, he passed a rickety wooden sign: *Buckets*. He saw one sitting under the sign, dust blowing off the top of the gravel. Rachel's.

So she was in front. And he was second.

Though he was so relieved to drop the weight, he was careful to use proper body mechanics in setting it down. He stood and stretched, then ran on, uphill but free of the burden. Although he was exhausted, lengthening his stride felt great.

He estimated himself to be about halfway through the long run. He hoped against hope he could finish it out, but another checkpoint stopped him and he was made to do fifty pushups. Then he ran about five hundred yards, where he was stopped and made to do fifty pushups with a twenty-pound plate on his back. Then he ran another five hundred yards, was stopped, and it was fifty pushups with a twenty-five-pound plate on his back. Eventually the weight plate maxed out at thirty pounds, and after two rounds, the plate weight decreased by five pounds, until he was on his last set of pushups without weight.

The entire time, the volunteers yelled at Evan, basic-training boot camp style. They yelled that he was a lazy slug, that his grandmother could do more pushups than he could, that if he wasn't so out of shape with cheeseburgers he could do these in his sleep, that if he thought about taking a break before this challenge was over, he might as well quit.

He lost count of the pushups after the third round. All he knew it was easily more pushups than he'd done cumulatively in his training in the last year in the Premier League. Maybe two years. The psych-out yells from the volunteers didn't bother him in the slightest because none of the insults were specific. They were general, designed to break people with lower self-esteem and in lesser physical shape. But he felt for the guys—and women—who'd get this far and have to hear this while pushing their bodies to the absolute limits.

He knew this psychological torture shouldn't have bothered Rachel either, but he didn't know what was in her past. He didn't know if they'd said anything that struck a chord of fear. But she wasn't here, which meant either she'd dropped out—unlikely—or she'd passed this part of The Golden Crucible and run on.

He lowered his knees for a second to take a deep breath. "Are your knees on the ground?" the volunteer yelled. "Are they? You want to start this set over? Get on your toes! Go!"

Evan was sure he could summon the strength to stand and clock this guy in the nose, but he was only doing his job.

When Evan got through the last fifty, he collapsed and drank water, and drank and drank. He wiped his mouth with this forearm. Sweat dripped from his brow into his eyes and they burned. His chest ached with every gasping breath he took. His arms were overcooked noodles.

"You're done," the volunteer said. "It's all downhill from here."

Evan nodded while trying not to roll his eyes. All downhill from here. He sincerely doubted that.

Five minutes later, he realized that it wasn't a light figure of speech. It was all downhill. Steeply downhill. Evan supposed he should have known that what went up must come down, but with all the pushups and sprinting, he'd forgotten he was at the top of a hill. He'd forgotten nearly everything.

He jogged carefully, touching occasional tree trunks for balance, turning sideways sometimes to navigate declines. He was sure there was a beautiful view if he could look up, but if he wanted to keep from falling, he couldn't take his eyes off the ground.

Which was why he was able to easily spot a bare leg

outstretched, trail sneaker on the path. He nearly tumbled ass over tin cup trying to stop his momentum-fueled descent.

"Holy sh—Rachel?"

The look on her face—he'd seen it a few times on the football pitch. Wincing pain and pale-white shock, laced with fear of having to quit before the job was done.

She wore an outfit similar to the one she'd been made to wear yesterday, only this one was hers. Black shorts with a charcoal-gray bra top. It showed her muscles, her curves, and her scraped-up dislocated left shoulder.

"Oh, no," he said, falling to his knees beside her. "What happened?"

"I fell," she said. "Down a stupid hill. Do you have any idea how many trails I've run? I've never fallen down."

"Well, that insane bunch of pushups was designed to weaken your body for the downhill run. We were all set up to fail here. This is no shortcoming of yours."

"I stupidly, *stupidly* grabbed a tree to stop my rolling after I fell. And I kept rolling and I yanked my—" She sucked air in through her gritted teeth.

"You dislocated your shoulder."

"I think so," she said. "I've never done this before."

"I have. And a few of my teammates have. It sucks. Are you waiting for help?"

"I haven't called for help."

"What? How long have you been sitting here?"

"About twenty minutes. I thought if I gave myself a little time to get used to the pain, I could keep going. But—ahhh," Rachel groaned.

"It's getting worse."

"Yeah. But I don't want to quit. I *don't* want to quit," she repeated as he shook his head. "Not after this far."

She was a fighter, but this insight was no revelation. "Okay," Evan said. "Look. I can help you, I think. I'm not a doctor, nor do I play one on the telly. But I've popped a teammate's dislocated shoulder back in for him. I can probably do yours. You're a lot smaller than he was."

"Do it," she said. "Tell me what to do."

"Hold on," he said. "Before you make this decision, you need to think about the options."

"I've wasted about twenty minutes considering my crappy options. I've been crawling two or three feet ahead on my knees every few minutes so the cuff doesn't ding me for inactivity."

He ignored her. "Okay, a dislocated shoulder isn't a grave injury but if I pop it back in, you could have mobility problems for a while, and I mean months, especially if you keep going now and lifting and climbing and whatever else you'll need to do for the next twenty-four or more hours."

"I can take a few months off from racing after this," she said. "I was considering it anyway. I've been racing for years, and maybe I could use a break."

"Your other option is to drop out. Wait—" He held up a hand when she vigorously shook her head. "You can drop out and ... I can give you the money."

"What?"

"I'll give you the money for your school tech lab. I'll donate it. Money isn't exactly an issue for me. I've done okay. Go take care of yourself, and I'll very happily write a check to the school. No one will owe me anything. You won't owe me anything. It would be my pleasure."

"No."

"No? Just like that?"

"No. What kind of lesson does that teach the kids?"

"I don't know," he said. "That there are nice people in the world?"

"It teaches them that a rich person needs to step in and solve things. It teaches them to rely on generosity instead of earning their way."

"Are you overthinking this?" he asked. "Isn't the end more important than the means?"

"No," she said. "I'm going to earn this. And if I lose, I'll earn that too."

"It's not shameful to bow out when you need to."

"I don't need to," she said. "A dislocated shoulder won't kill me. Pop it back in."

"It'll hurt," he said.

"It will hurt if I wait for an EMT or a doctor to do it, won't it? I'm not getting away with no pain. So just pop it back in now."

Evan hesitated. He didn't want to say he'd rather not be the one to cause her that intense pain.

"Please," Rachel said. "Please. I started this whole thing. It sucks. It's no fun. I'm tired. But I started this, and I'm going to finish it. That's who I am."

Evan understood that. Because that was who he was too.

"Right," he said. "Lie on your back."

Rachel sank to the ground, wincing.

"Are you right-handed?" he asked.

"Yes."

"That's good. I don't know what else is in store for us, but use your dominant arm as much as you can."

"I feel like I don't need you to tell me that, but I appreciate the advice."

Evan knelt by her left side. She was cradling her left arm close to her body, so he gingerly took her arm and extended it at her side. "I've only done this once," he said. "But it was on a guy who had had his shoulder dislocated before so he talked me through it. And I remember what I did. Try to trust me."

"I—I trust you."

"If this doesn't work or if I mess it up more, promise me you'll call for help."

"Just do it," she said. "I'll handle it."

"I know this sounds impossible," he said, taking his sneakers off, "but you need to relax. I have to try to get your muscles to give a little bit so the ball of the arm bone can move back into the socket. So the more you can physically relax, the better."

He guided her left arm away from her body to about

forty-five degrees. He braced his socked foot against her side, just under her armpit. Her arm tightened with anticipation. He took her hand and held it, rubbing his thumb over her palm. "It's okay," he said. "You're okay."

He let himself look into her deep eyes as long as she let him before she finally closed them.

The moment he felt her go slack with relaxation, he drew her hand toward him as firmly as he could, using his foot as leverage.

She cried out as the top of the humerus popped into the socket.

He went limp with relief. She searched his face. "Is that it?" she asked.

"Yeah."

She sat up, flinching, but her face calmed as she moved her arm around. "Still hurts like hell," she said. "But I can move. I can move."

"Good," he said. "Because that was the least *humerus* thing I ever had to do."

Rachel stared at him.

"Humorous?" he said. "The bone? It's a pun, like?"

"Let's go." She turned her head away from him, but not quickly enough to hide her grin. He was sort of ashamed at how happy her grin made him, but he'd never have to admit it to anyone. He reached out to help her guide her bag's strap over her bruised skin and settle the pack on her back.

"You're officially the most badass person I ever met," he said. "I'm not kidding. And I've met a lot of guys who are, and a lot of guys who think they are. You're head and dislocated shoulders above them all."

"Thank you," she said. "I mean it. I promise that when they interview me after I win, I will only say nice things about you."

"That's a relief," he said, pushing his feet into his sneakers. "Though I have a feeling you're a good winner. Not sure what kind of loser you are."

"A less good one," She started to jog very slowly and

cautiously down the hill.

He jogged beside her as she picked her way down. "There are a couple of guys not too far behind us," he said. "I want to pick up the pace while there's some room here to spread out."

"I'm sorry," she said. "I'm holding you back."

"There's no reason to," he said. "You're faster than me."

He was trying to say, *Don't be scared. Now that you've decided to stay in, don't stay in with fear. That's how you get hurt again. Be all in.*

She sped up to a run, then a slightly faster run, then an even faster run as her confidence returned. He followed.

***

Rachel had never run with someone before, alongside someone, keeping an eye on him while he kept one on her. Maybe for a little while, but not for this long, through so many miles and ordeals.

As they ran, their energy fed off each other's. When she was feeling weak, she let his breath beside her carry her through. When she felt him slowing down, she led him through with confidence until he got another wind.

Stride matching stride for miles, she learned the way he moved, the way he smelled, the way he breathed, what was difficult for him to maneuver and what was easy for him to dash through. Even when she pulled ahead of him and couldn't see him, or he pulled ahead of her around a bend and she lost brief sight of him, she was physically aware of where he was in space and how close he was to her. When they stopped for water and snack breaks, she felt his swallows without having to look at his throat. The cold water touched her lips and slid down her tongue the same way it did for him.

The shared physical experience was sensual, intimate, and raw. Rachel shook her head now, at a good pace on a straight path. Two men stayed close. Sometimes they overtook Rachel and Evan, and sometimes they fell behind, but they stayed competitive.

In the moments Rachel remembered they weren't a team, that Evan was her competition too, she tried not to think about it too hard. There was always tomorrow morning. This morning, she'd awakened about forty minutes before the alarm and allowed herself to absorb the heat Evan gave off. She didn't want to get up and go. Then she remembered the year she spent with her last boyfriend, and how she had been absolutely useless as an athlete that whole year, letting the relationship distract her from winning or even performing particularly well. Men were pretty good at blocking the road to success, deliberately or not. The longer she lay there, the more time she wasted. She'd had a chance to peace out, and she took it.

But here he was again, and here she was again, and she was in even deeper than last night.

"I keep staring ahead, squinting," Evan said, "to see the next checkpoint. But it's been a while."

"I know. I don't like it. When it comes, it won't be fun."

"Maybe we're wrong. Maybe it will be lunch."

"It's cute how you're so optimistic," she said. "My bet is we're not getting lunch."

"We didn't get breakfast. Would he deprive us two out of three meals? Especially when a lot of people probably threw up the last one with those pushups?"

"I'm not sure," Rachel admitted. "But I don't like that we have been allowed to run free for this long. Something's up."

Something was up. About ten minutes later, they were stopped at the next checkpoint and asked by the cheerful male volunteer, "Ready for lunch?"

Evan's only reply was a wary look. Rachel said, "No offense, but the last volunteer who greeted us with a smile made us do more burpees than should be legal."

"No burpees here!" he said. "That's a guarantee. I have your lunch right here. Chicken salad, fruit, electrolyte drink, even a macadamia-nut cookie. My absolute favorite, by the way."

He reached into a cooler and handed Rachel a wooden box covered with crisscross leather straps connected with bronze rings, and an elaborate filigreed lock on the front. The wood and leather were a bit damp and cold from cooler ice.

"Here you go," he said. "Your yummy lunch is right inside. All you have to do is open the box. There's a nice soft grassy area over there to sit on, under that tree. A perfect spot for a picnic."

The look on Evan's face when he took his box was as indecipherable as the puzzle appeared to be. "Great," he said. "I just love this."

"You have a whole hour break," the volunteer said. "A free hour that doesn't count against you. If you open the box fast enough, you can spend that time relaxing and eating. If you don't open the box in an hour, I'm afraid you'll need to give the box back to me. You'll be allowed to pass this obstacle but ... without eating."

Evan muttered something Rachel couldn't hear and stomped off to the little grassy field. He threw his box hard against the tree and it fell to the ground, unscathed.

Hadn't pegged Evan for the temper-tantrum type. "Aw, are you hangry?" she asked.

He grunted.

She felt his eyes on her as she set to work. She ran her hands along each strap and inspected each connecting ring. "Not only are we supposed to be athletes, we're supposed to be geniuses," he complained.

"I'm in Mensa," she said without looking up.

"Oh, hell. Of *course*, you bloody are."

"I can do this," she said. "And I owe you one now, so if I open it, I'll open yours too."

"Maybe I'll get it first."

"Maybe," she conceded. "You didn't sound very confident in your ability to do so, though."

"I'm not." He picked the box off the grass and sniffed it. Rachel stifled a laugh. "What?" he demanded.

"Nothing. I like that you're using all your senses."

"I'm trying to get some nutritional value out of smelling it. Since I probably won't eat it."

She ran her fingers along the front, back, and sides of the lock, and a panel flipped open, with numbers on three rolling barrels. A combination lock.

"You will. Give me a minute."

***

He gave her a minute, then twenty-nine more. At that point, Rachel was ready to throw her own box against a tree. The code had her baffled. She was smart, but she wasn't a trained codebreaker. Without any clues, she couldn't narrow down the number of combinations from infinite to less than infinite. She twisted each strap to see if any clues were on the undersides, but no luck. She considered cutting the leather straps with a Swiss army knife, but the rings connecting the straps would prevent opening the box. The combination code needed to be cracked, and she had no idea how.

"Okay," she finally said. "I'm at a loss."

Evan lay on his back on the grass. "I'm sorry. I'm preoccupied thinking of pints and chips at the pub. I can't concentrate. You said you'd do it."

"Argh, I can't," she said. "I was sure there was some way I could get around using a combination because we have no clues. I thought there must be another way to spring this thing. But if there is, it's about the most brilliant thing ever."

"I don't give Justin enough credit for crafting a puzzle that would stump a Mensa science teacher. He's more of a what-you-see-is-what-you-get guy."

"I agree."

"In that case," he said, "maybe it's something we've already seen. Any idea how many kilometers we've run so far? Or miles?"

"I could estimate it but there's no way for me to know without a phone app."

"Okay." He sat up. "What else have we encountered?"

"The monkey bars," she said. "How many were there?"

"I think six, plus six hanging balls, that was twelve."

"That doesn't give us a three-digit number."

"We did it ten times. Maybe one-twenty?"

She spun the numbers. "Nope."

"What about those damn burpees?"

"One hundred, three times. That's three hundred. Then three two-hundred-meter sprints. Nine hundred. That's twelve hundred total. But we need a three-digit number."

They looked at one another. "The pushups," they both said at the same time.

"I didn't count them," she said.

"Neither did I. We'll have to figure it out. They were sets of one hundred and fifty. First set was without weight. The second set was with twenty pounds. The third was twenty-five, then the fourth and fifth were thirty. Then we went back down, twenty-five, twenty, and then last one was no weight."

"Say it again," she said and counted on her fingers as he did. "Eight," she said.

They both stared into space a moment, then almost at the same time, grabbed their boxes, spun numbers, and then both locks popped open.

"Four hundred!" she said.

"I'm going to emotionally eat to forget I did four hundred pushups today," he said. "And we still have about twenty minutes to eat lunch."

"Great job," she said. "You're the one who cracked that."

"You would have."

"If I did, it would have taken me too long. Give yourself credit."

Evan smiled and Rachel knew that expression—the one

she'd seen on countless students' faces after getting an A on a test they'd lost sleep worrying about, proving a hypothesis they'd come up with in the lab, or winning a ribbon for their science fair presentation. It was hard to see because often the self-doubt came from zero encouragement at home, if not outright skepticism about their intelligence. This obviously intelligent grown man had doubted his own critical-thinking skills so quickly that his first impulse was to fling the box against the tree. His self-satisfied smile was great to see—before he stuffed his smile full of food, of course.

"This is really good," he said.

She didn't bother to fight the urge to shove food impolitely in her mouth. Politeness, civility—none of that meant anything anymore. Nothing meant more than the taste of a cold chicken salad, a banana, a cookie, and a now-lukewarm but still delicious fruit punch-flavored drink. She drank half the bottle in one swig and let the sweetness slide down her throat. "So good," she said.

"What's your favorite food?"

She thought for a moment. "My favorite food is a panini I once ate in France. It was literally an entire loaf of bread with prosciutto and cheese, completely flattened out in the press so it didn't feel like I was eating an entire loaf of bread. But I did. And I didn't feel well the rest of the day. But it was amazing because I ate it looking at the Eiffel Tower in the distance."

"I like that. I like that you didn't just say your favorite food. You had an actual favorite food experience."

"The Eiffel Tower is probably like a nothing thing for you, though," she said. "I imagine if you're from Europe, it doesn't have the mystique it has for an American."

"Oh, I don't know," Evan said. "I think romance is romance. It's universal."

Rachel busied herself packing up lunch wrappers so she could avoid his gaze, but when she assumed it would be safe to look up, he was watching her face. "What?" she asked.

"You know what."

"I think we analyzed it enough."

"Did we? Did it work for you? Your plan to eliminate the tension?"

No, it hadn't. It continued to build with every second she spent with him. And she continued spending seconds with him despite the fact it went against all reason. She wasn't his glamorous-girlfriend type. He literally admitted he shied away from commitment. This crackling something between them was a dangerous third rail for this race. He was a distraction from everything important to her, the reason why she was here.

"I'll take your non-response as a no."

"So what?" she said. "I mean, so what if it didn't work? We both know this isn't a good idea. I'm not the one-night or one-weekend type, so sorry to disappoint you there."

"What makes you think I am?"

"Well, you—" *You're a sports star. Isn't that the life male sports stars lead? Fans throwing themselves at you? Offering you things?*

Rachel was too tactful to say any of this out loud, but he got it. "That's not me," he said. "I've had girlfriends, sure, and most of them didn't last too long, but they were girlfriends I was loyal to when I was with them. I fully intended to commit to—" He stopped.

"Grace. It's okay. You can say her name."

"I fully intended to commit to Grace," he said. "I did. And then the time came to do it forever, and I couldn't. I'm as disappointed in myself as a human as she was. I didn't understand it any better than she did. But none of it was because I'm some kind of womanizer. In fact, if you talk to anyone who knew me in school, they'd tell you how uncool I was. Girls didn't fancy me. They all probably saw me in the tabloids years later and wondered what the world could possibly be thinking. I played football, and I didn't play well until I was fourteen or fifteen. I played because I loved to play, but I showed no talent early on at all."

"You dated Grace Regan," Rachel countered. "Whom I

had never heard of, I admit, until I Googled you, but she's Miss Thing in Great Britain."

"I did, but she didn't seek me out. My cousin knew her from somewhere and introduced us one night on a group outing. It's not like I could have snapped my fingers and she'd come running."

"You absolutely could have done that if you'd wanted to. You're hot and famous."

"*You* won't come running. You quite literally ran away from me this morning."

"I'm not remotely in your league of humans." Rachel stood and walked her trash to the barrel ten paces away. When she turned back around, Evan was an inch away from her. He leaned in, and his eyes held hers. She so wanted to look away. His gaze was emotional quicksand. But she couldn't.

"It's true," he said. "You are not in my league. You are so far above my league that I'm basically ignoring everything that is good for me—and everything good for you—to stay close to you."

She opened her mouth to answer, but he held up a hand and she bit back her automatic retort.

"I could be cute and say I don't know what it is about you," he said. "But I know exactly what it is. You're beautiful and superhero strong and Einstein smart, and I never met anyone with determination like—well, like me. I get you."

Rachel swallowed. Twice. "That determination will clash tomorrow, when one of us needs to win. And if you're trying to distract me—"

"If I'm trying to distract you, it will at least keep our playing field even because I'm so distracted by you, I now have to try to run with three legs."

Rachel's eyes widened, then she snorted with laughter. "Did you really say that?"

He laughed too. "Yes." Then he looked over his shoulder and his face grew serious again. "Look. The only reason I'm not kissing the hell out of you right now is because there are people around. But I plan on kissing you as soon as we're out of sight of the guys behind us. If you don't want me to kiss you, I suggest you run ahead now, and run fast, because if I get the slightest inkling from you that you want it too—"

He stopped, and she nodded.

She circled back to their camp spot and slid into her pack straps. Hot plain flashed across her shoulder and she gasped softly. "Damn it." It wasn't possible that upper-body strength wouldn't be called upon in the next day. Luckily, monkey bars, rope climbing, and pushups were in the rearview mirror, unless they would repeat obstacles. It wasn't the probable scenario, though, as The Golden Crucible was known for surprise elements. Justin was far more likely to have worked with originality from start to finish. Plenty of opportunities could come for this pain to get worse as the race wore on. Rachel's first-aid kit had ibuprofen, but not a lot of it. Her shoulder would likely feel worse before it felt better, so no point in wasting her limited number of ibuprofen pills yet.

Evan moved beside her and slipped his arms inside his own pack straps. Three runners now tried to get into their lunch boxes. They would be an hour at the longest, though, and Rachel wanted a better lead on them. Especially since Evan had suggested an unscheduled stop, and despite her better judgment, she would take that stop.

"Ready?" she asked.

Understanding dawned on his face. "I am if you are."

"Try to keep up."

She took off running, Evan hot on her heels.

***

Evan was hot everywhere. It was a hot August in the White Mountains today. The sun beat hot on his neck, his face, his arms. He was sweating in places he didn't remember sweating in the past: the insides of his elbows, behind his ears, his eyelids.

But he chased Rachel. More specifically, he chased her rear end. Her glute muscles contracted—one, then the other—as she pumped her legs. Her injured left arm swayed gently, but she pushed through the air with her right arm to get up small hills fast.

She led him at a very fast clip. She wanted to gain ground, and so did he. He wanted to gain enough ground for them to have a comfortable lead. So he would have enough time to kiss her the way he wanted to.

And, of course, so he would eventually win. But that long-game goal wasn't as interesting to him right now as his short-term goal was.

Rachel perspired as much as he did. A wet spot showed on the waistband of her shorts. The skin on her arms and her thighs glistened, and his groin ached with the desire to run his tongue along her lower back, from hip to hip, then up her spine. Then he'd kneel and kiss the back of each of her knees before licking up the inside of one of her thighs, pulling her shorts fabric aside with his fingers so he could reach as high as he could. He wanted to hear her moan. He wanted to make this fierce warrior surrender. He wanted her to give in to him completely.

She wanted it too. Evan was sure of it.

She wasn't trying to outrun him. Not yet, anyhow. Every now and then, she looked over her shoulder to gauge his distance from her. Each time, seeing him close on her heels, she appeared satisfied.

After a while, she slowed, slowed, slowed to a stop. She bent her knees, placed her hands on her thighs, and evened out her breathing. Evan did the same.

Then she turned to him. That little secret smile—

He closed the distance between them in three strides, put his hand on her good shoulder, and steered her off the path. He put a few trees between the path and them. They could see the path, but only the most observant of runners would think they saw Rachel and Evan.

She leaned back against a thick tree. Her eyes were heavy-lidded. Her lips parted.

He couldn't take it anymore. He put a hand on her cheek, and she turned into his touch ever so slightly, inhaling, closing her eyes.

He dropped his mouth to hers, not gently. She responded—not gently.

They tasted each other urgently, deeply. They clutched each other's hair, clothes. He dragged his lips away from hers and dipped his tongue into the center of her collarbone. It was as deliciously damp and salty as he'd hoped it would be. Her breath was ragged, and she reached her right arm over her head, scratching the bark. He spread his fingers around her waist, then ran a hand up. He slipped one finger underneath the band of her sports bra and looked at her, eyes seeking permission. She kissed him hard, giving it.

Still kissing her, he pushed his hand underneath the damp material and fingered the underside of her small breast. She squeaked into his mouth, and his lips curved up as he slid his palm higher and spread his fingers, cupping her entire breast. He flicked her nipple, then pinched it. She stopped kissing him and laid the back of her head against the tree. Her eyes rolled up, then closed.

He bent and caught her hard, tight nipple in his mouth, through her bra. She cried out, and the sound made him so hard, he thought it would crack right up the side. He desperately wanted to sink into her, to pull her on top of him and watch her amazing, strong body take her pleasure from him before he spilled into her.

A branch snapped, and they both froze. Rachel covered her mouth with her hand.

Not here. The noise was a chipmunk or something, but the interruption was enough to jolt Evan to his senses. He couldn't take her here, and not because they were jeopardizing their lead with every second they weren't racing, but because he wanted her to feel free, to feel like she could do anything to him and make any sound she wanted. He wouldn't exploit their weakness here. He would enjoy their weakness—tonight. Assuming they'd be once more rewarded with tents to sleep in.

"Rach—" he said.

"I know," she said. "Let's go."

She tugged her bra down, though she hadn't been uncovered. She ran her hands over her braid in an apparent effort to smooth away the passion of a few moments ago and bring herself back to the even-realer-than-normal world, where they had to fight through another day.

"Hey," Evan said. "To be continued?"

She nodded, but her eyes were on the path. She headed toward it, and he followed her.

CHAPTER 11

Rachel had to get away from this man. For her own good.

But he made it impossible. Every minute she spent with Evan, she liked him more. Every minute with Evan, her goal of giving a big gift to her students wasn't at the top of her mind. Every minute she spent with Evan, she could see herself with him after the race—next week, next month, next six months, and all the nights in that time.

He had admirably kept up with her so far; it was true. But she could lose him. She knew how to win a race, even a long, unpredictable one like The Golden Crucible. She should have been in front this whole time. Chatting during lunch held her back. Making out with him against a tree definitely held her back.

But then, a dislocated shoulder would probably have taken her out for good if not for his help.

Okay, he'd gotten her back up and running, but it was a fluke accident that wouldn't happen again. She had to get away from him if she wanted to win. She had to get away from him if she didn't want to run down the path of imminent heartbreak with a man who'd discovered—and clearly expressed—that commitment wasn't his thing.

At forty-five, Rachel was tired of men who couldn't commit to her. She'd dated on and off in the fifteen years since her divorce. Some men had lasted longer than others, and she'd had less fun with some men than others, but every man she had been with devolved the relationship into a competition. She was forced to compete over everything, and she was so over boyfriends being threatened by the things she wanted to do. She felt no particular pressure from family or friends to find "the one"—possibly because they all secretly thought she'd aged out of that possibility. She had given up the idea of finding a fairy-tale prince.

A handsome, kind, smart man who liked the same things she did, who looked at the world through a similar lens, who understood and wouldn't try to stifle her competitive spirit and devotion to her students. Someone who was into her.

Nope. Didn't sound like anyone she'd met lately.

Sigh.

They were running fast but easily, stopping every now and then for water. He kept pace beside her, and she checked him out in her peripheral vision every now and then. She tried hard to stay in her own head but she couldn't. Finally, she said, "What's your biggest flaw?"

"My biggest flaw?"

"Or weakness. Or whatever you want to call it."

"Searching for something to exploit so you can win?"

"Always. But that's not why I asked."

"Why did you ask?"

So I can have a bigger list of reasons to stay away from you. Though that no-commitment thing is a big one. "Just making conversation."

He laughed. "You have a strange way of starting conversations."

"Fair enough."

"What's *your* biggest flaw, superstar? Because from where I'm standing, you don't seem to have too many."

"I love to win," she said. "I think you figured that out, though."

"That's a flaw? A winning mentality?"

She slowed to navigate a rocky downhill, and he let her lead. "It's both a positive and a negative, as I'm sure you know from experience."

"You're probably right."

"I'm always right."

"I don't suppose cockiness is on your list of flaws."

"Well ... I'm not always right," she conceded after a moment of thought. "But I try to be sure of something before I say it so I'm right more often than not."

"Interesting."

"Because I hate to be wrong more than I hate to lose."

"Do you think," Evan asked, pausing to push a branch aside and ducking under it, "you might be putting too much pressure on yourself? With always needing to win and be right?"

"I don't always win," she said, "and there are situations in which I lose or I'm in the wrong. But I have a habit of setting the bar high for myself."

"What haven't you won? Well," he backtracked, "I know you lost the Prestige Race and that's why you're here. But I—I don't mean a race. I mean something else. Something more important."

"We all have lots of disappointments."

"Sure, but what stands out?"

Maybe it was physical weariness, or the pain in her shoulder, or her resurfacing hunger, but Rachel didn't have the energy to hold back. Anyway, he seemed to genuinely want to know. "I've found that many people—let's be honest, I mean men—want to compete over every little thing. And it's impossible to have a relationship that's equal."

"This has been a problem with some men you dated?"

"It's been a problem with *every* man I've dated. Granted, I haven't had a million boyfriends—only a few long-term ones and one marriage. Maybe it's not a big enough sample size, but I'm willing to postulate that either every man out there is unable to handle a woman being better at anything than them or they're not all like that but I have a knack for picking the ones who are."

"Give me an example."

"Just one? How can I pick?"

"Wow."

"I'm not kidding. It really is an issue."

He slowed slightly so he could bend over and scratch his leg. She paused with him, and sped up with him again when he straightened. "There's a lot of scratchy, itchy, uncomfortable stuff out here in the sticks," he said. "I like the controlled environment of the football pitch, and then I like restaurants and cars and urban things. I don't love this."

"If only your fans could see you now, whining about grass, dirt, and insects."

"Insects?"

She felt him turn his head to her but she kept her eyes on the path.

"What kind of insects?"

"Insects that bite and leave you itchy."

Evan muttered something Rachel couldn't hear. She smiled.

"Please take my mind off the bitey insects," he said. "You were about to tell me how your exes created competition with you over everything."

When Rachel trained, she ran alone, sometimes for hours. She never wore earbuds; she didn't listen to music or podcasts. She always felt like that took her out of competition mindset, distracted her from the moment and the feelings of fatigue, boredom, and frustration that she needed to feel to learn how to get past them.

But sometimes when she ran for so long, her brain wanted to bring up memories, turn them over, and examine them from every angle. It was easy, through physical exertion, to access events from her past. She'd never done it out loud before, with another person.

"You don't want to hear this," she said.

"I do," Evan insisted. "What are we doing, anyway? Just running for God knows how long before we're stopped and required to do something heinous. And I do want to hear."

She put out her fingers to lightly brush the velvety petals of a bright white flower as they passed. "The first example I can think of was high school. Maybe I should have paid more attention early in life to how guys could get in relationships, right? I'd known Nick for years before we started dating when we were juniors. One day we got in an argument over something we saw on TV, and one thing led to another, and it led to him saying he didn't think a woman could be elected president of the country because men wouldn't view a woman as authority. He took care to say *he* didn't believe that, but that most men did, and that meant a woman didn't stand a chance."

"What an idiot," Evan said. "But he was a kid. I'd like to hope he someday learned his lesson."

"Oh, he learned it that year, because he was in the midst of running his campaign to be our class president when I decided to jump into the race."

Evan laughed. "I take it you won?"

"Of course, I won. But he couldn't handle the possibility of a woman beating him, so he broke up with me about a week after I announced my candidacy. He already knew I'd win."

"Poor lad. I take it you did a great job as a madame president."

"I did do a good job, considering I didn't even want to be president. I didn't run for re-election."

"You ran to spite him, then?"

"Well, he threw the challenge out there. He made it a competition."

"Interesting," Evan said. "But then, you were young. As was he."

She looked at him long enough to see him cross his arms in front of his torso, grab the hem of his sweaty shirt, and pull it over his head.

Eyes on the road, girl. Who knew if he was trying to distract her or if it was innocent, but either way, she wouldn't have it. She increased her pace a bit.

"Then," she continued, gaze resolutely ahead, "there was the time after college when a guy I'd been dating about a year, Mitch, got obsessed with this game called Go. It's a board game of strategy that originated in China. Anyway, I knew nothing about it, but someone taught him how to play and he got into it, joining clubs and going to tournaments. He told me he wasn't all that good at it, but he was improving and he loved it."

"Good to have a hobby."

"Agreed. I thought I should take a little interest in it. After all, he loved it, and I thought maybe it would be something we could enjoy together. I decided to read up on it and watch some videos on strategy. I surprised him one day by suggesting we go to his club meeting together and I could try it."

"I feel like I know what's coming next."

"I won a few games. Well, I won all the games I played. And his new friends asked me to join a tournament because they thought I'd have a great chance. How could I possibly have known that was the tournament Mitch had wanted to be invited to?"

"Ah. He got mad because he thought you were glomming on to something that was his."

"He got mad because I was good at it. I offered to show him what I had learned, to help him out, and he broke up with me."

"Fancy that."

"He said it 'wasn't working out' but I knew that was the reason." She dragged her forearm over her sweaty forehead. "I'll give you one more: my ex-husband. With him, it was the worst, and it wasn't one thing. It was day after day."

"What do you mean?"

"He was constantly trying to show me how to do things the way he did them. He thought he had the right way for everything and that I was a hopeless dummy."

"How could he think the smartest person he ever met was a dummy?"

"All I know is no matter what I did, he said he had a better way: a better way to wash dishes, a better way to organize the bookcase, a better way to make a scrambled egg. When I told him what I was doing was perfectly fine, he would go to the Internet and try to find the expert 'right' ways to do these things so he could show me he was right about, like, everything."

"Was he ever right?"

"I mean, neither of us was wrong. There's more than one way to scramble an egg. If it tastes good at the end, who cares? But he needed to be right about something every day. He needed to be better than me at everything. It was exhausting."

"Maybe taking his advice once in a while would have been—"

She turned her head and narrowed her eyes at him.

"A nice gesture," he finished.

They ran in silence for a few minutes. Rachel had a bad feeling in the pit of her stomach—a feeling of having failed at something, of having made a mistake, but it wasn't a familiar feeling for her, and she didn't need to explore it right now, not while she was trying to win big at something. "Well," she finally said, "it wasn't why we got divorced. We had a million other problems. But that everyday chipping didn't help."

"I understand."

She slowed to a stop and pulled out her water. "How did this happen?" She took a long drink, swallowing once, twice, three times. Evan looked at her throat the whole time, and she didn't want to let on she'd noticed. "Didn't I start out asking you what your flaws were? How did I end up telling my whole story?"

"I guess I'm just sneaky." He shrugged.

She sat on the grass. "And what about you? No flaws?

You're perfect?"

"No," he said. He remained standing. He dropped his pack and slid his shirt back on. Rachel didn't know if she was relieved or disappointed.

"If there's something I'm not, it's perfect," Evan said. "You're not a football fan, so you don't know how aggressive I was on the pitch. I tried to be as nice as I could off the pitch, in interviews and such, because I was a right bastard when I played. I didn't want to hurt anyone. It wasn't personal. But I wanted to be in control of the match every minute I was out there. I was physically aggressive with opponents and I yelled at my own teammates a lot."

"Yelled at them?"

"Encouraging them, but it sounded angry when I did it. Most of them understood, though, so it was okay, but when I see videos of me yelling in matches, it makes me cringe. My voice doesn't sound like mine, and my face doesn't look like mine."

"The fans love you, though," she pointed out. "From what I could see yesterday. The guys all acted like you were the god of socc—football."

"Fans like aggressive players. They can live vicariously through it. Most people don't yell and shove their bosses and co-workers around for hurting them or insulting them or taking credit for their ideas or winning a promotion over them, but when they see me pushing and yelling, it's like I'm doing it for them."

"And the more they loved it, the more you did it?"

"Not quite, but it certainly didn't discourage my behavior."

"I haven't seen you do that here," she said.

"What, be a jerk?"

"Or emotionally aggressive. I mean, you're obviously fighting through this race, but you're doing it methodically. You're not fighting me. Or anyone else."

"Well," he said. "I probably should. And in the next few hours, I will start to. But I'm not a star at this kind of competition, whereas back then, I was good at what I did. It's been better here to pace myself and learn, so when my big push comes, I'll know what I'm up against."

"You're up against me."

"Believe me, I know, and it sucks. And you—you're shifting my priorities. More than a bit. And I can't let that happen, but I'm letting it happen anyway."

Rachel fell silent. He'd articulated exactly what she felt inside, said it for both of them.

"I can't lose," she said.

"Neither can I."

"One of us has to."

"As strongly as I want to win, I'm starting to realize that I just as strongly don't want to see you lose because I know what you're doing this for," he said.

"I feel the same. Whatever happened with Grace, even if it was your shortcoming in the relationship, you didn't deserve to be maligned in the public like that. I know what you're doing this for too. If I weren't in this race, I'd be rooting for you."

"So would I. For you, I mean."

Rachel stood. "We're in each other's way. I'm moving ahead."

"Maybe I'm the one who wants to move ahead."

"Then run faster than me." She put out her hand. "Good luck. May the best woman win."

"That doesn't seem sporting of you."

"Sorry." She was sorry. Maybe that meant she was losing her edge. She could consider it in therapy long after this race. Not today.

He took her hand, and she instantly wished she hadn't offered it. She wanted to pull his hand toward her, lay it on her cheek, or her breast, and feel the heat of his skin on hers. She wanted to kiss him. She wanted everything to drop away so they were no longer in the woods, in New Hampshire, in this world. Somewhere with no consequences.

Instead, she squeezed hard, her usual finger-smushing

handshake. "Cheerio, Evan."

"Seriously?" he asked with a smile. "Okay. Cheerio."

She was still holding his hand when the blow to her chest knocked her down.

CHAPTER 12

Rachel's body flew back a few feet, and she landed hard on the ground, blinking.

Evan's body froze in place.

"Did…" she said, confusion distorting her face, "did I just get shot?"

She put her hand on her chest, and her hand came away red. "What?" She looked dizzy.

Evan moved. He crashed to his knees beside her, leaning her against a tree and running his hands over her. He felt her abdomen and chest, slid his hands over the material of her top. "It's not ripped." He smeared his fingers in the red liquid and looked at them. "Paint," he said. "You got hit with a paintball."

A loud splat came over their heads. Red paint streaked down the tree trunk she was lying against. "They've got paintball guns."

His vision darkened for a moment with rage. The red paint wasn't the only red he saw. This was a game, a race, a sport, but he'd seen fear in Rachel's eyes and felt fear run through his veins, if just for a moment. He would throttle these stupid volunteers. Or Justin, if he ever made it to the end of this nightmare of a race.

"It's okay," Rachel said. She took a deep breath. "Ow. That really hurts. Ohhh, my shoulder."

Evan rushed to stand and help her up. He'd just held out his hand when a paintball smashed into the back of his thigh, and his hamstrings burned. "Damn it!" he yelled. "I thought Justin said he was concerned about liability."

"We signed a waiver," Rachel said. "I'm pretty sure we agreed to this."

Another paintball whizzed by Evan's right bicep. A voice sounded from behind them. "Get hit three times and you're *out!*"

Evan hauled Rachel up by her uninjured arm. "Run," he said. "Run!"

Rachel did, and so did he.

They heard the paintball guns firing, but they dodged the hits before coming into a clearing. A wide-open space covered in wild grass. The paintball gun toters stepped out from behind trees.

Exposed and surrounded, Evan and Rachel didn't hesitate. They started to flee across the field at top speed. Paintballs splattered around them.

"There's like a half-dozen of them," Evan panted. "How many people does Justin hire? This is insane."

"We need to split up," Rachel said. "I'm going left. You go right. As far from me as you can. Then they'll split their forces and we each have less chance of getting hit."

"Okay," he said. "And run in a zigzag. Run crazy."

"Yup. Go!"

They diverged paths, and he saw at least two gun-wielders take aim. He zigged left, zagged right, ducked a few times, stopped, and changed direction as often and unpredictably as he could. Paintballs shot by him, exploding on ground impact.

Then they chased him.

How far would they take this? They had other runners to torture. But if Rachel and Evan were far enough in the lead right now, maybe the shooters figured they could take their time messing with them.

Evan heard Rachel shout from far across the clearing. "Rachel!" he called. Should he hang a left?

A pause, then he heard, "Go! I'm okay! Go!"

He was torn.

Okay. This wasn't real. No one would die. Rachel might get shot in her bad shoulder, and if that happened, Evan would beat the crap out of the guy who hit her, but that was still part of a big game. It wasn't real. The worst that could happen was one or both of them could get eliminated. If he didn't concentrate on getting the hell out of here, that would be his fate.

Rachel had made it clear—and he knew damn well himself—that they had no business together. During this race or beyond. If he was ready for commitment, he lived in another country, one he intended to return to and repair his career. Even if she, what, came to London? Unlikely. But in that fantasy, the press would drive her crazy. She wasn't glamorous, wasn't famous, was—gasp!—older than he was. Assuming they ever cared about Evan again, they'd never leave Rachel alone, and she didn't deserve that.

This paintball attack wasn't real. It was a game. What was real was his desire to run and grab her. Instead, he kept running away because Rachel had been right.

It was time for them to go their own ways. For their own good.

***

Evan squinted up at the sun through the mass of greenery overhead, trying to gauge the sun's position in the sky. Ugh, it was no use. He wasn't a Viking. He couldn't understand direction from the sun's position, nor could he figure out the time of day. He wished he'd thought to pocket the little alarm clock he was given last night. Ancient or not, it would have at least anchored him in the present moment.

He shielded his eyes. The sun seemed to be slowly arcing

to his right. Which must mean that right was west. In August, he could count on some extra hours of sunlight, but it would be extra hours of being lost.

He was lost.

He'd lost the trail when he veered right, away from Rachel, and in zigzagging away from the paintball snipers, he must have knocked himself off the trail. He'd tried for what seemed like an hour to find a trail marker and came up empty. He attempted to use the position of the sun to keep going in the right direction to avoid losing ground and circling, but at this point, he had to concede he didn't know where the hell he was going.

Trees, rocks, brush—it all looked the same. An occasional clearing, but he couldn't tell one from another. He listened for running water but heard none, so there was no river to follow.

Finally, he sat and took a deep breath.

He had a bottle of Magnitude, eight protein bars, and zero cell phones.

Nighttime wasn't here, but every minute was a minute closer, and he wasn't exactly the rough-it sort. If he sat in place longer than his allotted time, he knew Justin's crew would come to fetch him, but then his race was over.

Which, in the end, might be better than them finding his skeleton licked clean by a bear. Or a mountain lion? Or a big bird of some kind? Maybe he should have read up on New Hampshire wildlife, but he'd anticipated well-marked trails and at least minimal supervision. He hadn't expected to be chased off the path in a bloody panic by a bunch of Fortnite wannabes.

He hadn't expected to be alone. Or he had, but then the race started, and he'd gotten used to company, in the form of one badass woman and her ninja skills.

He was an athlete, not a survivalist. This was crazy.

Okay, he could do this. He could call for help if he had to, but that would mean his now-publicized race would end with tabloid headlines such as, *Footballer gets lost in woods, calls for rescue.* The whole point of this stupid event was to reinvent his reputation as a stud, not to look like a dolt and plummet it further.

He examined his surroundings. Maybe if he sat for a moment and got his bearings, he could figure it out. But one tree looked like another, didn't it?

He could close his eyes for a moment. The sun was so warm, the rustling leaves were the perfect white noise, and his body was so, so weary. Just, like, ten minutes of rest. Then he could pick a direction and keep going—

"Hughes!"

He shook his head, eyes still closed, mind still drifting. Squirrels, chipmunks, little songbirds were singing him to sleep. So peaceful...

"Hughes!"

He startled and sat up. "What?"

"Over here!"

Evan turned his groggy head to the right and saw a figure in his old jersey jogging slowly toward him. What? Where was he? Were they winning? Another concussion? He couldn't have another one, he didn't want to have to take a break—

"Evan Hughes!"

Evan rubbed his eyes. Right. New England. The Golden Crucible. Lost. Rachel—but here was his football fan, the one who'd come to HQ to cheer and sing before the race began. The man ignored a respectful spectator's distance and instead came over to him.

"Listen, mate," Evan said. "I don't know what you're on about, but—"

The man pulled a cold water out of his backpack and handed it to Evan, and he grabbed it without hesitation. He drained half the bottle in one pull. "I'm Ray. I see you went off on your own. You must have a good plan, a secret plan."

Evan shook his head. "I have no plan. I took a wrong turn. I have no idea where I am. I could be halfway back to The Golden Crucible HQ for all I know right now."

Ray's face fell. "Oh. I thought you had a winning strategy. Like in that match against Liverpool in 2019, when you—"

"Don't," Evan said, holding up a hand for a fraction of a second, then dropping it as soon as he realized it required an unexpected amount of exertion. "I have no plan," he reiterated. "I'm sorry to disappoint you. I'm just reacting now. I reacted to the last obstacle by running as fast as possible away from it, which was what I was supposed to do actually, but I went too far."

"That sounds familiar."

Evan raised his brows. "What?"

"I mean, it's what you've been doing for a while now, isn't it?"

Evan narrowed his eyes. "Explain."

"Running away so you don't keep taking hits. Running fast and ending up where you don't feel comfortable."

"I'm uncomfortable with a fan being able to analyze me better than my therapist. To whom I pay a lot of money, by the way."

"Well, I'm your biggest fan, so…" Ray trailed off.

"So … what?"

"I don't know. I sounded creepy."

Just now he was realizing that? "Do you know where we are?" he asked Ray.

"Sure," Ray said. "I have GPS."

"I don't want to cheat," Evan said, "but can you at least point me in the right direction?"

"The reason I asked you if you have a plan is that you took a shortcut. I thought you did it on purpose."

"How could I do it on purpose? I don't know where I am. They took my phone. I have zero sense of time or place. It's Saturday, right?"

"You should drink the rest of that," Ray said, nodding at the water. "Dehydration can make you hallucinate."

"I'm not sure *you're* what I would hallucinate." Evan finished the drink in two swallows. "You said I took a shortcut?"

"Yes, and it's not against the rules, as far as I know, but if you don't get back on the trail soon they might send someone to take you out of the race. You really should get back on track. I can lead you."

"Thanks, mate. You're all right."

"You helped me. I'm glad I have a chance to help you."

Evan furrowed his brow. "How did I help you?"

Ray turned. "Come on." He walked, and Evan followed. It was equally possible that this guy would lead Evan to the race path or he would lead him to an unmarked white van and abduct him, but at this point, Evan figured either was better than sitting here disoriented.

"Five years ago this month, I was diagnosed with colon cancer."

Evan didn't know what he'd expected Ray to say next, but it definitely wasn't that. "I'm sorry, mate."

"Don't be. I'm in remission. But at the time, I felt alone. I'm single and my family is across the country, and I didn't want to put them out or worry them, so I was alone a lot of the time. And I spent that time watching European football."

"Football?"

"Yes. I never much got into American sports, but European football was always on in the hospital when I was having chemo. I started watching it, and I was hooked. I watched a ton of matches. When there were no live matches to watch, I streamed past matches online. And you were my favorite player."

"Thank you. I mean that."

"What I liked was how nasty you were on the pitch."

"Yeah," Evan said, remembering what he'd told Rachel. "A lot of people liked that."

"But you were so genuinely nice in interviews. It made me realize that I could be mean and tough when I had to be. And right then in my life, I had to be."

They arrived at a race trail marker: a red arrow on a white

birch tree. "I want to say thank you, because without you—
"

"Don't thank me for that," Evan insisted. "I wasn't the reason you beat cancer."

"Well, no, of course you weren't," Ray said. "My drug trial treatment was the reason I beat cancer. And the amazing nurses and doctors."

"Um, right. Right."

"But," Ray added, "you inspired my attitude. I walked into treatment every time like Evan Hughes would, intending to kick its butt and make it sorry. And I did. I can't believe I can finally repay you now."

"You didn't owe me anything. But I'm happy you helped me because I would have not been kicking butt sitting on that rock by myself until it got dark."

"You kind of dropped off the radar last couple of years," Ray said. "I wondered what happened to you after you retired and all that stuff with your girlfriend. And then a friend of mine who works for The Golden Crucible told me you'd entered. I only live a few hours from here so I decided to come and root for you. What are you doing after this?"

"After the race? I don't know, I guess getting a good night's sleep."

"I meant, are you going back to the UK?"

"Well," Evan said, "should I?"

"I don't know. You have a ton of options."

"Maybe fewer than you'd think."

"I think you helped me without even knowing it. Someone like you—you can help lots of people. With your talent and your name and your money. Just something to think about." He looked down the path. "That woman got lost also. She was wandering around a different area than you. But she's back on the path now. My friend texted me. You're ahead of her right now, I'm pretty sure. Someone got ahead of you both, but I don't think she's far, if you get a move on."

"Is she okay?"

"Who?"

"Rachel. Is she okay?"

Ray paused, examining Evan's face. "You like her!"

"She's a very impressive woman. She's hard not to like."

"No, I mean you *like* her like her."

"Shut up."

"I'm sure she's fine. But please don't let her win," Ray said. "Don't let feelings for a chick get to you."

"Ah," Evan said. "It's too late for that. Don't tell anyone, Ray." He put out his hand. "You're a good friend. Thank you."

Ray shook his hand. "Chicks, man," he said. "They'll ruin you. But then, you knew that. Cheers." He performed an odd little salute before trudging off the trail and out of sight.

Evan took a deep breath and ran. But he looked over his shoulder every few minutes for Rachel.

***

Evan felt a little sad nostalgia when he reached the next checkpoint without Rachel. But that nostalgia transmuted into fear—and defeat—very quickly.

A pair of male volunteers in swim trunks greeted Evan with high spirits at what appeared to be the mouth of an interesting but not particularly threatening-looking cave. The cave was actually man-made, they told him, with shrubs and brush added to blend in with the rest of the forest. It was the most elaborate of The Golden Crucible setups that the runners would face.

"I run through this?" Evan asked.

"Nah," one volunteer said, the one with blue mirrored sunglasses. "You swim through."

Panic gripped Evan's heart. He tried not to change his expression. "Swim?"

"Yeah," the other volunteer said. He had spiky hair that was the result of artful mousse-ing. "In the dark. It's awesome. It's like you're in outer space."

"If outer space was wet," his partner said.

"You don't think there's, like, humidity in space?"

"Dude, you don't swim through humidity."

"Dude, haven't you seen videos and stuff of those guys floating in space? The closest thing I've come to that was in a pool. How do you know it's not wet up there?"

"Dude, because astronauts wear space suits, not bathing suits."

"Dude, that's the stupidest—"

"Dudes," Evan cut in. "I need you to explain this to me a little better."

"Sorry," the sunglasses guy said. "If you have a headlamp, you should use it when you first go in, so you can see where the water begins. But then you'll want to store it because water will ruin it. As soon as you get to the edge, you can jump in. Don't dive in headfirst, but you don't want to try to wade in, because it's deep."

"How deep?" Evan asked, and he was sure his heart paused its rhythm to hear the answer.

"Ten feet."

Damn it. Damn it. "How far is the swim?" Evan asked. "It can't be that far."

"About three hundred meters."

Evan tried hard to force his mind to process the information without the interference of his emotions. His fear. But it was impossible. He stared at himself in the blue mirrored sunglasses. He looked like a nervous Smurf. "Three hundred meters of swimming in ten feet of water in the dark." It wasn't a question, but he was hoping against hope one of the guys would correct him.

"Dude, you got it," Spiky said.

Evan must have looked grim because Spiky added, "It's amazing, bro. It's like those flotation tanks, except you have to actually, you know, swim. But it's peaceful. Zen."

"Will I just hit a wall when I'm at the end?"

"Nah," Sunglasses said. "The water will glow with light

so you'll know you're near the end. As it gets brighter, it will get shallower until you can walk out of the water. Then it will be nice and sunny."

"This doesn't feel—" What could he say that wouldn't give him away as a wuss? "Totally safe. If ... you're someone who isn't a great swimmer. Or easily disoriented."

"There are volunteers at both ends," Sunglasses said. "And there are two lifeguards inside the cave. You won't be able to see them, but they will be able to see you with night vision goggles. They probably won't see you're Evan Hughes, but they will see your body if you run into trouble. And if you yell, they will be able to easily hear you and come help."

"Remember, though," Spiky said. "If you get help, you're out of the race. But they are there in case something goes wrong."

So if he passed out or thrashed around, they wouldn't know it was the famous athlete. Until they dragged him out. Not very comforting.

"You're lucky you got here a couple of hours before dusk," Spiky said. "We close this obstacle at sunset and when we do, runners are stuck on this side until tomorrow. We'll bring them food and tents, but they will lose enough ground that they're sure to lose the race. Lots of people go home at this point."

"Yeah," the other guy said. "People have been dropping out today but this spot narrows the field."

The Golden Crucible might be short one English footballer at sunset as well. "Cheers," Evan said in a very *un*cheery voice as he headed to the mouth of the cave.

"Enjoy, dude!" one of them called.

Enjoy.

The mouth of the cave was nondescript and kind of boring. But knowing the challenge it held inside, it would have been more appropriate if the entrance resembled the gaping maw of a bloodthirsty tiger, or the angry roar of a dragon.

Evan stopped to pull his headlamp out of his pack and secured it on his head before stepping inside.

It was dark. He'd been told it would be, but experiencing the absence of light was chilling and claustrophobic. Once he snapped off the lamp, he wouldn't be able to see his hand if he waved it in front of his face. There was zero source of light in here to allow the human eye to use to adjust to night vision. He'd legitimately see nothing.

At the age of eight, Evan had ventured into a lake on a summer day to feel the cool water around his ankles. He was a city boy, and his parents were city people too, who couldn't swim and didn't have enough disposable income for swimming lessons for their only child. They'd warned Evan to stay away from deep water. And he'd intended to.

But they weren't there that day, when some lads from down the road rushed Evan in the water, lifted him, carried him to the center of the lake, and threw him in the deep center. He struggled and fought and cried until one of them realized he couldn't swim. They all dragged him out, apologizing, then fled before they could get in trouble.

Evan's fear of water was real, and in thirty years, it hadn't subsided.

He did learn how to swim eventually. He'd hired a personal coach about ten years ago to teach him. He knew the basics to swim a few laps. When he'd entered The Golden Crucible, he had been mostly confident he could perform short-term water challenges like the ones he'd heard races like this had: swim to a little island or duck underneath a submerged wall—all quick, here-to-there-type challenges.

None of the races he'd researched had a long swim in water over his head. In the dark.

He couldn't do this. He absolutely couldn't pull this off.

There was no way. His time standing here would be well spent crafting an excuse to get out of here and drop out of the race.

But he had come so far. He *could* swim. He knew how.

He just didn't want to. He was too—scared. Too effing scared.

But the press. The publicity he'd basically wanted to do this for. He'd look like a right idiot if he dropped out because an obstacle was too scary.

Evan wished he could be carefree and dopey, like Sunglasses and Spiky, and enjoy this for the relaxing, zen, peaceful time they said it was. But when it came to swimming, he wasn't normal.

Evan didn't know how long he stood there. He knew one or two lifeguards could see him standing there. He hoped they couldn't see his teeth chattering, his body shaking.

But he wasn't cold.

A five-foot walk led to where the water began. Evan moved forward like he was walking the plank.

Wasn't he?

When he was about six inches from the edge, panic rooted his feet into the ground and sprouted up through his legs, rendering him immobile.

Water in his mouth, his throat, his nose, his ears.

I can't swim! I can't swim!

He couldn't do this. He couldn't do this.

"Nice day for a swim."

CHAPTER 13

Evan whirled to face Rachel, blinding her with his headlamp.

"Yo," she protested, shielding her eyes with her forearm.

He didn't apologize; he just angled his headlamp up and turned back to the water. Rachel raised a brow.

Something was up.

"Sorry I caught up to you," she said. "But—have you been standing here for a while? The guys out there said you came in here like ten minutes ago. You should be near the end by now."

"No," he said faintly.

From the back of his head, Rachel knew something *was* up. When you ran for hours alongside someone, you learned their body movements, their body cues. Even in the small bit of illumination they created, she saw he was off.

"You'll probably want to take your sneakers off, right?" she asked, kicking her own off. "And your socks. Nothing more disgusting than wet socks. And I'm running out of dry clothes."

She dropped to her knees, slid her pack gingerly off her bad shoulder, and secured everything in the waterproof pockets inside. When she had finished, Evan still hadn't moved.

"Evan," she said, and when her lips formed around the syllables, she realized she hadn't said his name aloud very many times. It was foreign in her mouth.

"Let's go," she said. "Unless you want me to get a head start. But at this point, that's not wise for you. I'm not sure why you've been wasting time—"

She cut herself off when he turned and stared at her like a zombie.

"I can't," he said.

Rachel stood quietly for a minute, taking in the fear on his face, illuminated by his turned-up headlamp. "Do you know how to swim?"

"Yes."

Okay, so technically *can't* didn't mean *can't swim*. Which was positive, because she wouldn't have been able to drag him for three hundred meters, even if her shoulder wasn't a hot painful mess.

So, the *can't* was something mental. In a competition like this, a mental block was much harder than a physical limitation. A strong mental game could give you what you needed physically. But the toughest athletic body in the world couldn't work with a mind full of fear.

If she went ahead now, if she left him now, she was sure she'd win. The few racers who had been ahead of them had interchanged since the beginning and there was no clear-cut top contender. Evan was it. And this would take him out.

She was going to win. But she had to go now.

She could hear his teeth chattering. It wasn't cold.

This was it. All she had to do was jump in and swim, and this race would be hers. The money would be hers. Fifteen minutes of fame would be hers, even if she hadn't particularly wanted it.

All she had to do was go.

Go.

How could she leave him like this? He could have left her to suffer her dislocated shoulder, but he helped her. He could have let her be afraid when the scary invisible volunteer told her to not move, but he'd called out immediately that he was there. He could have left her to sleep in the cold on top of her broken tent, but he'd—

Damn it. *Damn* it. This was an opportunity for her. This was an opportunity to reach her goal. This was an opportunity to leave behind a guy who was no good for her anyway. All relationships deteriorated into competitions in the end, after all. She could make sure she won this one. All she had to do was *go*.

Evan backed up a step.

She pushed away her logic, her instinct, her own needs. She'd regret this. She would.

"Evan," she said, "we're going to do this together."

He took a deep breath, but it was raggedy and short. He was listening, though, which was a plus.

"I'm going to stay with you," she said in a confident, calm voice. "You swim in the dark the exact same way you swim in the light. And swimming in deep water is the same as swimming in shallow water. Either way, your feet are off the ground. How far away the ground is doesn't change your strokes."

He was listening.

"Take your sneakers and socks off and pack them up. Your shirt too. Keep it all dry. Headlamp too," she said, and after a moment, he did. Slowly, but he did.

It wasn't an appropriate moment to admire his muscled torso, so she didn't. She could do that on the other side. When he finally clicked off his lamp and zipped it up, they were in darkness.

"Okay, honey," she said in the same calm, strong voice. She reached out and laid her hand on what felt like his shoulder. "We're going in the water together. We can do this in less than ten minutes. It might feel like longer, but it's only ten minutes. Right?"

Evan nodded.

"I have to swim slowly," she said. "The breaststroke will

147

probably be the least hard on my shoulder, so that's what I need to do, but it's slower. I'm going to pace myself and go easy, and you'll be right beside me. Swim any stroke you're comfortable with. If you need a break, we can stop and tread water for a bit, but remember if we keep going, we'll be done faster. Every stroke will get us closer. I bet there's dinner and tents on the other side."

He nodded again. It was eerie to see this strong, aggressive athlete caught in a panic attack like one of her students on advanced-placement math exam day, but no one in the world was immune to fear.

"I'm going to talk the whole time," she said. "Or sing, or something, but you know I'll be right next to you every moment."

It seemed she was getting through to him. She hoped so, because if he panicked halfway through and grabbed her, he could put them both in danger.

"Remember you said I'm the most badass person you know?" she asked. "You're right. I am. I'm going to get us both through this. You're going to owe me so majorly."

She couldn't tell in the darkness if he smiled faintly, but she was almost sure he did.

"Like I said before, nice day for a swim," she said with a return smile. "Let's go, Hughes. You and me. You got this. We got this."

She took his hand and moved with him to the edge. "One, two, three!"

They slid in and were immediately submerged. Rachel tried not to let go of Evan's hand until they could bob up and start swimming. She hadn't expected the water to be warm. The darkness was disconcerting—no, it was scary. It was. But she flipped the off switch on her emotional reactions and turned her logical mind way up. She drifted a bit to the left, but she ran into a wall of vertical ropes. She was sure they were on Evan's right also, designed to keep swimmers moving ahead in a straight line so if they became disoriented, they didn't move in exhausting endless circles.

They resurfaced and she felt the droplets hit her face as Evan shook his head. She let go of his hand and smoothed her fingers over her scalp, but her braid remained in place. "Come on," she said.

She pushed her arms from her chest to begin the breaststroke. Her shoulder burned the way it had been since she'd convinced Evan to pop it back into place, but the warm water seemed to soothe the joint and muscles somewhat. If she was alone, she'd be able to do this easily.

But she wasn't alone. She paused in her stroke to make sure she felt Evan swimming beside her. His movements were choppy, splashy, so she said, "Stay calm. No need to waste energy. Just move through the water. You know how."

He settled his stroke down and they moved side by side. She remembered she'd told him she'd keep talking, so she did. She told him about her two little cats at home, Azrael and Mayhem. She told him about the time her older brothers threw her a surprise sixteenth birthday party, but it was filled with all their friends and they forgot to invite any of her friends. Which was how her first boyfriend turned out to be her brother's best friend and he was embarrassed for the duration of their three-month relationship.

She tried the entire time to talk softly so as not to expend too much energy, but loudly enough for him to use the sound of her voice as a beacon. Every now and then, her fingers grazed the rope wall, keeping her on track.

When she started to feel like a real nerd telling him her silly stories, she asked, "Are you okay?"

"Yes," he said in a voice closer to his usual strong one.

"Do you need to stop?"

"No."

Rachel had half wished he'd say yes. She was weary, and sore, and her thoughts were a tangled mess.

She broke into song to keep them going. She had never been able to carry much of a tune, but she sang the Alphabet Song, Happy Birthday, and Twinkle, Twinkle, Little Star.

"Like a diamond in the sky…" The lyrics faded in her throat as her eyes took in the faintest of light glowing in the water a few feet ahead.

"Do you see that? It's over, Evan."

The glow grew brighter and bigger with every swim stroke. Soon Rachel sensed the water around her growing shallower, even before she dropped her feet and went vertical. When she felt the ground rise up, relief washed over her heavier than the water had.

Evan beat her back to dry land and out of the cave by a few strides. He collapsed on the soft grass. He turned his head and looked this way and that, then lay on the ground. He bent his knees and swished them side to side. His breaths lengthened and grew calm. He closed his eyes.

Rachel waited a moment to let regret sink into her heart and mind.

It didn't. He lay in safety on solid ground. The muscles in his face lost their tension and she didn't regret anything.

She shivered, but the warm sun began to absorb the moisture from her skin. She only had one pair of clean shorts and a tank top left. She pulled her towel out of her pack. It was still a little icky, damp, and dirty from the night before, but she patted dry as much of her skin as she could.

She didn't want to guess how disgusting she looked and smelled right now.

He didn't smell like anything but perfection. How could that be? Maybe they smelled exactly the same so her nose couldn't pick it up.

She shoved her towel in her bag and carried her clothes behind a cluster of trees. Why were sports bras so impossible to take off when they were wet or sweaty? Wasn't the point of wearing a sports bra to do something that made you sweaty and damp? The gymnastics required to remove a sports bra were challenging for any woman. But her once-again screaming shoulder forced her into Cirque de Soleil-worthy contortions. She groaned and finally peeled the stupid thing over her head.

Dry and comfortable, she went back over to where Evan sat. He had propped himself up on his elbows and was looking back into the cave. When he caught her movement out of the corner of his eye, he turned to her.

"Are you sorry it's over?" she kidded. "Do you want to swim back?"

"I wouldn't have done it."

"Sure, you would have. Come on."

"I wouldn't have done it without you."

She didn't ask him why he had been afraid. He'd been vulnerable enough without her needing to know more about it. If he wanted to tell her some other time, he could. But there had been enough about that cave—darkness, deep water—to trigger myriad long-held phobias and nightmares for lots of people. Big, strong men weren't immune.

"You would have," she insisted, plopping onto the ground beside him. "You might have stood there for a while trying to gather up the courage. But you wouldn't have let this stop you. You'd come too far."

"That's exactly what I was thinking, that I'd come this far, but I was thinking of how I was going to handle the humiliation of dropping out because I was afraid."

"I think you'd be surprised," Rachel said. "Everybody's afraid of something. If you gave an interview and said you quit because you were scared, maybe some jerks would think whatever about you, but you'd get more fans out of it because people can relate to fear, to phobia. Frankly, people can't relate to someone who's a star professional athlete. They can root for him, but not relate in any way. But they can relate to a regular guy who's scared of something. Everyone knows how that feels. And you would have been respected for saying it."

"Well," Evan said. "Maybe you should have told me all that on the other side. Because then I could have gone home. Your advice is too little, too late."

"But didn't it feel great to face your fear?"

"It feels great now," he confessed. "But it didn't feel

great while I was doing it."

"What were you thinking? While you were swimming."

"I was thinking how you said it would only be about ten minutes. I was thinking about how warm the water was and how if someone would turn a light on and let me just float, it might have been spa-like. I was thinking that I hoped the lifeguards didn't recognize me, and if they did, that I wasn't giving them any indication that anything was wrong. I was also thinking you have the worst singing voice ever."

Rachel feigned affront. "What?"

"Like, the worst."

"It can't be that bad."

"You are completely tone deaf. But," he added, holding up a hand and halting her imminent protest, "I was also thinking your singing was the best thing I'd ever heard in my life."

Rachel swallowed. She should look away. She should walk away.

She should *run* away. That was what she was supposed to be doing, after all.

His eyes were green. No, brown. No. Green-brown? No—

She didn't know how his face had gotten so close to hers. "I liked your stories, too, your memories," he said. "Thank you for sharing them with me. What you did to get me through that—"

"You got yourself through that," she said. "I didn't pull you. I didn't push you. I only swam next to you. You swam the whole thing yourself."

"You would have won," he said. "You would have won, Rachel. All you had to do was move forward without me."

"I know."

"Why didn't you?"

"Don't ask me that."

He reached out a hand to touch her cheek, or the back of her neck, or somewhere, but she'd never know because she backed away. "Don't kiss me."

He froze. "Don't?"

"No, don't. Because nothing has changed. It wasn't a magic cave. We didn't go in with these obstacles between us and come out with them eliminated. Everything is still the same. And if you kiss me—when you kiss me—"

He seemed to hold his breath, waiting for her to finish.

"I can't do what I'm supposed to do," she ended. "And neither can you. We're distractions for each other. We're not making each other better."

"You got me across three hundred meters of mental torture created when I was a little kid, and right now I feel like Captain America for having done it. I pushed your arm back into the socket—despite my better judgment, I might add—because winning this race is important to you. We're making each other better. This weekend we are, anyway. I don't know what can happen later, but we've established a good partnership. You don't think so?"

"You know, at this time tomorrow, one of us will have won. Or neither of us if we keep getting distracted with each other and let someone else get ahead of us. But hopefully one of us will have won, and the other one will be headed home with nothing to show for all this. And so one of us will have handed the other that disappointment. I don't think that's a good start to a relationship. Or whatever."

"Maybe we're making this race bigger than it needs to be. Is it that important?"

"My students are important. Your career is important. I don't want to start rationalizing," Rachel said. "I don't want to throw away an opportunity here for a guy. That's not responsible."

"Running The Golden Crucible is responsible?"

"In that cave, you were why I did what I did. I thought about myself and my safety and my injury and my strategy. I thought about all of that. And I put it all aside. And I don't regret it, and I'm wondering what's wrong with me."

"All I could think about when I got lost in the woods was you," Evan said, "and where you were, and if you were okay."

It was what all women wanted to hear from the man they cared about. That he cared back, that she was his priority and his preoccupation. Why did Rachel want so desperately to run from it?

"Just—don't kiss me now. I still have to win. I can't do what I need to do if you do."

Evan parted his lips, but a reply didn't form. He simply nodded and picked up his pack. "I have no sense of time or distance or direction right now," he said. "But I'm willing to bet there's some kind of food happening for us soon. Hopefully we won't have to balance a ball on our noses in order to be allowed to eat. I'm kind of fried right now, and I wouldn't mind a bit of a break."

Rachel was dizzy from the abrupt subject change, but it was what she had asked for, after all. "I could use a break too," she said. "If I had my phone, I'd call for a pizza right now. Though I wouldn't know where to ask them to deliver it."

"Outside the creepy nightmare cave in Where the Hell, New Hampshire."

"What do you like on your pizza?"

"Anything. Sausage, pepperoni, black olives, mushrooms, onions."

"Pineapple?"

"No, that's disgusting."

Why did everything he said confirm him as the man she'd been waiting to meet?

Except for the no-commitment part. *He's not the one, Rachel. He's not even a one if there's no future.*

She followed him away from the cave and back into the woods.

***

They followed an unspoken agreement to hike for a while instead of running. Evan's body felt wrong, like he was trying on someone else's human suit and it wasn't comfortable in the legs, in the arms, in the back of the neck, and around the ribs. Everything hurt and body parts seemed to rub against other body parts that weren't anatomically close enough to rub.

Running through The Golden Crucible was beating Evan down.

He'd honestly thought this would be a test of endurance and speed and agility. He'd assumed that when the race was over, he'd need a few weeks off to rest, but he hadn't counted on feeling this used-up before he finished. They had less than a day to go, but it didn't feel good that more of the race was behind him than in front of him. He didn't feel strong. He didn't feel anything except weariness, soreness, and the overwhelming desire to pack it in.

He could blame it on not having stayed in peak physical shape since his retirement, but he'd been training pretty hard for this. Fitness was his lifestyle, and he hadn't let it go to pot since leaving the Premier League.

For not the first time in the months he'd been training, his age crossed his mind as a factor. He wasn't able to deal with as much as he used to. He was far more fit than the average thirty-eight-year-old man, but he wasn't number-nine striker Evan Hughes anymore. Not quite.

Age hadn't slowed Rachel down. At forty-five, she was more physically fit than any woman he'd ever met half her age. Her weekend-warrior dedication had made her strong, capable, sexy— He shook his head, then peeked out of the corner of his eye to see if she'd noticed he'd done it. She hadn't. She looked resolutely at the ground ahead, spotting every rock and twig and root so she wouldn't stumble.

Maybe it wasn't age for him either. Maybe he was simply tired. But he only knew how to be a footballer or talk about football. Getting tired now wouldn't help him stay relevant to his former fans, or possible new fans.

Middle age was a weird, unknowable thing. Was it a time to relax into what you already were and build on what you'd already done? Or was it a time to reinvent yourself, start something new that you didn't have the wisdom or the money for before?

The idea of reinvention was scary, especially when you were a man whose previous incarnation had been so successful. How could he move into an Act II?

Why was this race messing with his head? Why couldn't he finish and execute his previous plan?

Because his previous plan hadn't accounted for Rachel and how she could very well beat him and knock his plans to heck. How he'd be thinking about her for a long, long time after someone won a medal tomorrow.

"Look." Rachel pointed up the hill they had started to ascend.

"Checkpoint," he said. "I have a feeling we both hope it's dinner."

"I do."

"What do you really hope it's not? What could they ask us to do up there that would have you considering dropping out?"

Rachel was quiet for a moment as she thought. "Upper-body-strength stuff," she said. "Anything where I'm going to have to deadlift, or monkey bar, or carry something enormous like an atlas ball."

"Your shoulder hurts, huh?"

"I've been managing it with ibuprofen," she said, "but I haven't been taking much of it because I don't want to run out of it before I'm done and I don't want it to bother my stomach."

"But you didn't answer my question. It hurts?"

He could tell she didn't want to answer. She didn't want to admit a weakness despite the fact she had gently dragged him through his own weakness and didn't make him feel bad about it for one moment. "Yes," she said, perhaps recognizing her hypocrisy. "It really burns. Tomorrow I may head to the ER on the way home, or go Monday, depending how bad it feels."

"I'm sorry."

"Why are you sorry? You helped me."

"I'm pretty sure the doctor will tell you I didn't even remotely help the situation."

"What don't you want to see at the top of the hill? What might make you quit? The answer should be nothing, you know. It appears you conquered your fear in the cave. Anything they give you now is a piece of cake with buttercream frosting."

"It's not a specific thing they could give me now," Evan said. "It's if they give me anything other than a plate of food. I feel so bone-tired right now, all I can manage is food and sleep. I think a sleeping challenge would be ideal."

Rachel chuckled. "I could give you a run for the money in that event."

"Olympic-style napping."

"Freestyle snooze event."

Evan sighed as they trudged up the hill. He looked behind him every now and then; on this hill, they had a clearer view of the path behind them. "I don't see anyone back there," he said.

"Some people might have gotten tripped up at that cave," she said. "Or took some time to rest afterward. We already had a pretty good lead."

"I'm worried about getting too comfortable though."

"So am I. It's the rules that we have to rest for six hours, but it's not a rule when. We—you—I have to assume that someone else can get ahead in the morning."

He wanted to call her out for running from him this morning, but what would that prove or solve? They had no commitment. To each other. She'd had every right to run her own race today. He'd caught up to her was all.

When they neared the top of the hill, and the scent hit Evan's nose, he froze mid-step. His mouth watered. His eyes teared up, and he didn't know if it was the acrid smoke that did it or the joy of what the scent was.

He turned to Rachel, but she was still too, her eyes

closed, breathing deeply through her nose.

"You smell that," he said.

"Steak," she said. "On the grill."

"I no longer care if there are one hundred ninjas with nunchucks up there. I will destroy them all for a steak."

"I'm right there with you."

He liked how that sounded. She'd said it in the cave, too. *You and me.*

They broke into a run, following their noses.

***

Dinner was great—it *was* steak, and baked potatoes, and fresh garden salad. The antics they'd had to engage in before they could receive dinner, however, had not been so great. A huge maze of wobbly ropes and climbing walls and instructions to not let one foot hit the ground. It had taken nearly an hour to complete, and Evan had completed it a full five minutes before she had, but the pain had bloomed wider and wider at her shoulder with every uncertain step. Normally, she was a good climber, but having to rely on upper-body strength hadn't been fun.

Evan had waited for her, though. She didn't know how to feel about that anymore.

They hit the tent-and-alarm-clock checkpoint together, traveled about a mile further, and set up side by side. She'd said goodnight to him with a little wave, and now she sat at the center of her tent, getting cold.

She was about to slide into the sleeping bag when she heard a whisper.

"Knock, knock."

What was she supposed to do? Say *go away*? *Go away because I like you just a bit too much to let you into what is essentially my bedroom?*

She crawled to the flap and pulled it open. "Knock, knock?"

"Well, how does one request entry into a tent?" Evan

asked. "There's nothing to knock on. There's no doorbell. *Can I come in?* sounds, I don't know, creepy."

"It's fine." She moved aside to let him duck in.

He stood bent over, unable to stand his height upright. He looked around her tent, which she guessed was exactly like his. "Can I sit?" he asked.

Rachel nodded to the floor of the tent, not trusting the inflection that could happen in her voice if she said, *sure*. She didn't want to come off like she wanted him here.

Because she absolutely didn't want him here.

Yes, she did. A hum went through her veins and arteries, threatening to bubble up through the skin of her arms and legs. She caught herself wondering how she looked, and immediately cast the thought aside as it was a certainty that she looked like someone who hadn't taken a shower in two days, and who'd spent that entire no-showering time covered in mud and sweat. Long strands had escaped her braid, having been caught in barbed wire and disheveled in sleep.

"I don't know about you," Evan said as if he could read her mind, "but I am embarrassed at how spoiled a human I am. There are so many poor souls who don't have the luxury of doing a stupid race like this and calling it a personal challenge because discomfort is all they have every day. But me, two days without the comforts of a basic hotel room, and I feel like whining for an hour about it. I'm the worst."

"I want a bath," Rachel said. "With bubbles."

"I want a beer," he countered.

"I want to watch a *Gilmore Girls* marathon."

"I want toilet paper."

"I want a cup of hot tea."

"I want my bed."

"I want your bed too."

Evan blinked and raised his brows.

Rachel stammered, "I meant *my* bed. My bed. I meant to say, I want my bed too."

"No, to be honest, you do want my bed. It's the best

thing in my flat. It's got perfect sheets, perfect blankets. When you sit up, the pillows puff right back up to full floof. That bed's got everything anyone could want."

Including you. She felt her face getting hot. She was grateful for the darkness falling fast. "I'll take your word for it."

They sat in silence that was... *Uncomfortable* wasn't the right word. It wasn't uncomfortable. They'd spent long periods of silence together on the last day, and they were accustomed to being alone with their thoughts, together. It was more now that the silence was charged, like a live wire that under no circumstances should Rachel approach.

She sensed that Evan felt it too. He shifted his hips on her sleeping bag.

"I should go," he said. "I just wanted to see if you were okay."

This time, Rachel raised a brow.

She supposed he could see her skepticism in the dark because he confessed, "That's not true. I guess I wanted to say goodnight. And maybe—goodbye. I don't know. I suspect you'll get a head start on me again at dawn. I don't know what's in store for us tomorrow, but we'll be grinding it out most of the day. When we come down to the wire, we won't be in friendly chitchat mode."

They both paused.

"Okay." Evan made a move to stand up.

"Evan," Rachel said. "Wait."

He stopped. He didn't step any closer to her, and she appreciated that he respected her previously stated desire for distance.

Distance wasn't what she desired, when she'd said it or now.

Rachel Angel on her shoulder whispered, "I know what you're thinking. Don't. There's no near future because you need to beat him. There's no long-term future because he doesn't do commitment. There's nothing here for you."

Rachel Devil on her other shoulder whispered, "He's

into you. He's hot. He's a good guy. Why does everything need to be exactly right? Be wrong for a while."

Rachel resisted whispering, *Get off my shoulder. It's still killing me.*

"Is your shoulder okay?" Evan asked.

"What?"

"You're leaning your head into your shoulder. Is it okay?"

Rachel Devil giggled. Rachel pretended to flick a bug off her shoulder and sent her construct flying. "It's fine. Well, it's not fine. But it's passable. I'll get done whatever I have to get done."

"I have zero doubt."

He moved toward the flap again, and she repeated herself. "Wait."

She stepped closer to him and tilted her chin up to look into his eyes. He met her gaze, and she forgot where she was, what she was supposed to be doing.

"I may be tired and not myself," he said, "but I'm getting crossed signals from you. You said very clearly not to kiss you. But any other time in my life, when a woman looked at me the way you are, I—" He licked his lips. "And it's not even fair of me to compare you to anyone else I've ever kissed, because you're different. You're like me and the opposite of me at the same time. I have no idea how to stay away from you, but I said I would, so I—"

"I changed my mind," Rachel interrupted.

He drew in a sharp breath, then pressed his mouth on hers before they could talk themselves out of it again.

She wrapped her arms around his back and trailed one hand up his spine. Then she slid the hand under the hem of his T-shirt and duplicated the motion. So hot. His skin was so hot it was almost feverish, and she let her other hand follow the first.

His hand cradled the back of her skull, seemingly trying to pull her deeper as he plundered her mouth with his warm tongue. She melted into his mouth, into his hands. She'd been strong for hours and hours. She let herself go weak.

He must have felt her sway because he placed both hands on her buttocks and lifted her hips to his. She wrapped her legs around his hard torso. Her pelvis ground against his, and she felt the hard, heated length of him under the flimsy material of his warmup pants. Heat pooled in her lower belly, then flowed even lower, between her legs. She gasped at the sudden wetness there, so fast and so intense.

They never stopped kissing as he walked her over to her sleeping bag, kneeled, and laid her down on her back. He pulled away from her lips to unzip her jacket and groaned when he found only her bare skin. She'd pulled off her tank and shorts earlier to keep them dry for tomorrow, and thanked herself for thinking ahead so she could feel this, feel him, now. He parted the jacket lapels and let them fall open, exposing her to his admiration.

Rachel had always considered her body a long-term project. Years of running, lifting heavy, obstacle-course racing, and eating clean had chipped away at her excess, revealing a body that worked hard for her. It rarely let her down. It functioned at a high level. But in the last few years, she'd come to see and feel her body as a well-crafted, talented machine. She knew others thought she looked good, but that wasn't the goal, especially as she'd had it with dating recently. But as she looked down at her skin, her breasts with pebble-hard nipples, her belly, she shivered with being turned on—turned on because Evan was turned on by her. She was turned on at once again experiencing how her body could not only work for her; it could bring her pleasure.

Evan dropped his head and licked the hollow of her throat. Rachel fought the urge to moan, to cry out, because they weren't alone in the night. He traced his tongue in a jagged, moist trail down her chest, between her breasts, then along the underside of each. Rachel stuffed her knuckles into her own mouth and bit down with a squeak. His thumbs grazed the side of each breast, then he pushed her breasts together and kissed the cleavage.

Her skin was electrified. Her wetness felt like a gush as he brought his mouth to one nipple, pursed his lips, and breathed on it. Her exhales were heavy. She thrashed her head from side to side with frustration, and as she grabbed a fistful of his hair to either get him away from her or pull him into her, he caught her nipple between his teeth and tugged on it.

She crashed her fists onto the sleeping bag underneath her as he released her nipple and swirled his tongue around it until it was so wet. When he took his head away, the cold air bit at the wet skin and the sharpness of it was so good, so—

Then he did the same with the other nipple.

Rachel didn't know how long she could stand this. At the same time, she would have been happy to never get up again.

He sat up, reached behind him, and pulled his shirt off in one sweep. Night shadows played across the defined muscles of his arms, his pectorals, his comically perfect six-pack. She ran her fingers along the lines, dipping and rising. Finally, she pushed her fingers under the waistband of his pants and wrapped around the root of him, loving the way he dropped his head back, let his mouth fall open a bit, and took in the sensation of her touch.

After a few moments, he slid her pants over her hips and bent over her belly, dipping his tongue into her navel before moving lower. He dragged her pants down over her thighs and knees and abandoned them at her ankles. She used her toes to push them away from her.

He parted her inner thighs with his palms and kept them there as he bent over her.

She didn't want to close her eyes. Instead, she propped herself up on her right elbow and watched him as he tasted her. The sensations were overwhelming. He'd lick her in one direction and she'd feel it in her foot. He'd lick her in another direction, and she'd feel it in her inner arm. It was as if every nerve ended and began between her legs. As he drank her in, she felt the tension and the pressure build.

This wouldn't be a long, arduous task for Evan. She had been ready to come for him before he'd kissed her tonight. Maybe even before he'd kissed her last night. She felt that little click, that little clue her body gave to indicate she was on her way to an orgasm. She did lay her head back then and closed her eyes. Then she let the rush come over her sore, weak, tired, and thirsty body. It exploded in a burst. At its peak, she maybe not so gently pushed his head away, her nerve endings too sensitive and aware to take any more.

He laid his head on her stomach and held her as the waves came and went. Then she sat up, pushed him upright, and tugged his waistband down.

He asked in a whisper if she was sure. She asked if he had protection. Of course he did because, even in the middle of the woods with few belongings and fewer opportunities, men always did. And that was settled.

Then he lay next to her on the sleeping bag and drew her on top of him, caressing her shoulder lightly so she'd know why he chose this position. She planted her hands on either side of him, on the squishy sleeping bag, and hovered her hips over his as she kissed him. His lips, his chin, his cheeks were wet with her, and it smeared on her face as she tasted the mixture of her and him.

She rubbed herself on him, up and down, slowly—so slowly. She kept it up until his hips rocked and bucked underneath her in hot impatience. She paused with the tip of him at her entrance, then she took him into her with one hard, sharp movement.

She covered his mouth but he made a small noise under her hand as his eyes rolled up and closed. The skin of his neck pulled tight as he arched his back and pushed as deeply as he would go, filling her. She stretched around him and the feeling of being so full of him was almost too much to take. He grabbed her hips and moved her, and she matched the rhythm he started—long, hard strokes that threatened to draw another orgasm out from deep inside her.

He was on the edge of coming. She could tell and, not wanting to miss the chance, she sped up to bring herself along for it. He bit her fingers in an effort to keep peace in the night, and he came, hard, fast, and his throbbing sent her over the precipice as well.

She fell onto his chest, and he dropped his arms around her lower back. They lay there for a long time, not moving, not speaking, just breathing into each other.

Eventually, Rachel was cold, and she extricated herself to put her fleece pants and jacket back on.

Evan watched her, then also hurriedly dressed. "Do you want me to stay?" he asked.

"Um," she said. "Do you want to stay?"

"I wouldn't have asked you if it wasn't something I wanted. But I don't want to—overstay my welcome."

"I'll set the clock. But I don't want anyone seeing me and you leaving the same tent."

"I noticed when I came over here that our closest tent neighbor is around the bend. I think we'll be okay."

"Then ... yes. Okay. Yes."

"I'm going to get my sleeping bag and my pack. I'll be right back."

"Don't—"

"I won't use my headlamp. I'll be stealthy."

He slipped out, and she felt very suddenly alone. A few minutes went by, minutes in which she allowed herself to play back in her mind the memories they had finished creating. Before she could regret her decision to let him sleep in her tent, he returned and they spread one bag open on the ground and pulled the other one up and over them. She curled her back into his front, on her uninjured shoulder, and he wrapped his arms around her. She noticed he wrapped them around the center of her body, away from her sore spot.

He whispered in her ear, "You know, if we sleep naked, the heat will—"

She elbowed him in the ribs.

"Oof," he said. "I'll be a gentleman."

After a few moments of quiet, he whispered again. "You're going to run off in the morning before I wake up, aren't you?"

She sighed. "Yes."

His puff of exhale was a humorless laugh. "I'll catch you."

She winced, and not at the thought of him catching her. It was at the thought that she really, really wanted Evan Hughes to catch her.

She'd let him get to her.

She needed to run.

He tightened his arms around her, and she held his forearms.

He kissed her hair.

Tomorrow. She'd run away tomorrow.

CHAPTER 14

Evan woke up before Rachel did.

She was facing away from him, in the same position she had been in when they had fallen asleep, so he couldn't see her face. But he heard her relaxed breath.

Oh, no reason to be delicate about it. She was snoring. But it was a cute, soft snore, and it felt so good to be with her in her rare vulnerability. She was Superwoman by day, but a mere mortal in slumber. He liked that she'd let him into her world, even if she would wake up running.

Waking up before her had been one part luck, one part intention sent up to the universe. Before he'd fallen asleep, he'd set the intention to wake up first and before the alarm went off, and somehow, his unconscious body had cooperated. His arm was completely numb, but he didn't want to shift it for fear of rousing her. He tried to keep his breathing slow and even so her body didn't sense a change in the environment. He wanted to keep her here as long as he could.

He wouldn't have been so possessive, would have let her wake up and run with the new sun, if he knew for sure he'd be with her the next night. And the next night.

And a lot of nights after that.

He didn't trust himself, though. Since discovering he was Mr. Non-Commitment, he'd shied away from dating for fear of putting himself in that situation again. Women didn't want a flake, a just-for-now guy. They wanted a guy who had the potential to be everything. And he didn't have that.

He didn't. He hadn't had that with Grace.

But damned if he wasn't thinking long term about Rachel. About making plans and taking vacations and running races as a team, and living together and—

What? No. He didn't think that way. Evan Hughes wasn't that guy.

He'd thought he was that guy. Until he was inches away from engagement and the future. He'd not only disappointed Grace; he'd disappointed himself. He'd thought he wanted a partner, and there he was, rejecting Britain's most sought-after bachelorette like he'd had any right to.

But Rachel. Often ornery, often witty, always determined. Grace had been a lady; Rachel was a warrior, and Evan was drawn to her in a way he hadn't been with Grace, with anyone.

Rachel stirred, and Evan dropped his eyelids, deepening his inhales and exhales. She very slowly inchwormed out of his embrace. He let his arms go slack so when she rolled free of him, they dropped to the sleeping bag. He kept his eyes closed, sure she was looking for any signs of his wakefulness. When he didn't give her any, she unzipped her backpack at about a quarter speed, the zipper moving quietly on the track.

Evan risked opening his eyes about a tenth of the way, and saw through the slits that she was changing. He closed his eyes again. It would be bad form to see her naked without her consent. Though at the thought of that perfect tanned body, he felt himself growing hard and achy. He hoped she didn't glance down at the sleeping bag covering him.

When she was done and had tied her sneakers, she

slipped on her pack and crawled out. The moment the flap dropped closed, Evan sprang up and pulled off his sweats. Last night, when he'd gone back to his tent for his bag, he'd quickly dressed in today's gear under his sweats so he wouldn't waste a single second. He stuffed his things into his bag and bear crawled to the tent flap.

He peeped out and saw no one. He wanted to make good on his promise to Rachel to not let anyone see them emerge from the same tent—and frankly, any rumors would probably reflect just as or more poorly on him as on her. But no one was in sight. No tents were set up near theirs, so the coast was clear.

He counted softly backward from ten. When he got to one, he sprinted out onto the trail.

She wasn't getting away from him. Not this time.

***

Evan saw Rachel a couple of times, saw the flash of her white T-shirt on the trail some feet ahead, but he tried to hang back enough so if she looked over her shoulder, she wouldn't see him.

He couldn't be sure they were in the lead. The volunteers had told him last night that a good thirty people were left in the race, but most of them had slowed down considerably, exchanging their outside chance of winning for the satisfaction of finishing the race at all.

Evan wished there had been no press conference, that no one would care if he walked off the trail and went home. But if no one cared, it wouldn't be able to restart his career as was his intent, so he had to be grateful.

It was early. He had a good shot of being on top right now. He could ask at the next checkpoint, since the volunteers so far had been quite forthright with information about who was in the lead and how many people were left. It would have been otherwise impossible to know.

Just as he was thinking of the checkpoints, a small cabin

came into view at the bottom of the small hill Evan was descending. It didn't appear particularly threatening and didn't seem to contain a frightening or impossible challenge. Though after the hell cave of water, Evan was sure nothing else they threw at him—no matter how physically difficult—would rattle his mental game. He was strong now.

He slowed his pace, hopped up the two creaky front steps, and pushed open the door.

The large room smelled like wood and was a bit humid from the sweaty athletes who were sprawled on the floor in pairs, bouncing little balls, sweeping their hands across the floor, cursing, cheering.

Jacks. They were playing jacks.

More runners had been ahead of him than he'd hoped. Half a dozen runners in three pairs were playing, and one runner was waiting and watching.

Four of the players were burly guys, and sitting on the floor the way they were looked difficult for them without adding fine motor skills into the mix. Their hands were clumsy; jacks got smacked about and scattered, and the balls bounced out of control over and over.

Two women were each paired with a man. Rachel concentrated but wasn't too stressed out. Evan watched her a moment as she competently bounced the ball once, swept a pile of jacks up with one hand, and caught the ball. Her opponent shook his head. The other woman played across the room. Evan recognized her as the one who'd expertly braided Rachel's hair before the race. She looked in her element here, sweeping up jacks, laughing at the distraught look on her opponent's face.

A young man with glasses and a clipboard came up to him. "You've played jacks before?"

"I'm thirty-eight," Evan said. "So, you know, it's been about three decades."

The volunteer pushed his glasses up the bridge of his nose with his middle finger. "All right, real quick. Flip a coin to see who goes first. When it's your turn, toss the jacks in the air and let them scatter in front of you. The first round, you bounce the ball once, pick up one jack, and catch the ball in the same hand. Then drop the jack into your other hand and pick up each jack the same way. When you're done with your round, the other person goes. On your next turn, you pick up two jacks each time you pick up the ball. On your next, pick up three jacks each time—pick up the odd remainder at the end. If you miss, like the ball bounces more than once or you drop jacks or don't pick up the right number, you lose your turn and have to stay on the same number for your next turn. The first person to successfully make it to ten wins the round. To get out of this cabin, you need to win three rounds. Each round you lose, you earn an encumbrance to run with when you leave here. If you lose three rounds, you're docked thirty minutes."

Evan blinked. It was the last day of the race. One minute could be the difference between first and second place, never mind thirty minutes.

"I'm docked half an hour if I lose three rounds of jacks?" he asked, for unnecessary clarification.

The volunteer looked impatient. "Yes. There's a bench outside to wait on." He gestured to the runner who was standing alone. "This is your partner. Get to it."

He handed Evan a bag of jacks and a multicolored rubber ball. He handed his opponent a coin and pointed to a quiet corner. They hurried over and folded themselves onto the floor.

Evan couldn't help glancing over at Rachel. A damp lock of hair had finally escaped that tight braid and it brushed her forehead as she hunched over the jacks.

Then he studied his opponent, a guy about his age with a receding hairline and very defined biceps. The hair poking out of the neckline of his loose muscle shirt had a few stray grays.

Evan didn't know this man's story, or his name. But he knew that if he won three games of jacks, this man was effectively out of contention.

This was the first challenge where runners had the opportunity to blow others' chances out of the water. It was all well and good to do the challenges up to now, where you were really only responsible for your own performance. But half the runners who walked in this cabin wouldn't run out and hit the trail. They would walk out and sit on a bench, knowing every minute that passed stacked up into an insurmountable obstacle unless the front-runners somehow completely collapsed.

Evan used to love competition. He was pushy and loud on the pitch. He had no issues psyching out the other team and playing to win. Someone had to lose and every time he played, he played to keep his team on top. When his team won, he didn't feel bad for the losing team because they didn't feel bad for him when they beat him. That was competition.

Evan waited for that confidence, that competitive spirit, to rise up in him now. After a moment, he realized it hadn't, and it wouldn't.

This guy in front of him was just a guy. He hadn't been one of the top athletes spotlighted at the press conference; he was just a guy who'd made it this far. For Evan to keep going, he'd explode this guy's chances.

The guy put out his hand. "Travis," he said. "Nice to meet you, Hughes."

Evan nodded.

"Flip," Travis said, handing Evan the coin. "Heads."

"Tails," Evan said, and flicked the coin into the air. When it landed in his hand, he smacked it onto the back of his uncovered hand and revealed it. Heads.

"I'm going to try to beat you," Travis said, reaching for the bag of jacks, "and if I do, I confess, it will be the moment of my life. But if I lose, at least I'll be the one in the race who was beaten by Evan Hughes, and I can take that."

The woman who'd braided Rachel's hair squealed and jumped up. Her opponent flopped onto his side on the floor in defeat and shouted, "This is a damn *girl's* game!"

She patted him on the shoulder and ran out the door, flashing Rachel a thumbs-up on the way. Rachel's smile back was bright.

Evan turned back to Travis and trained his focus on the jacks and ball. "Go on," Evan said. "Do your worst."

***

Two rounds later, Evan was sweating like he never had. He used to play with fans screaming for him and against him, and threatening literal and figurative death at each other, and he never sweat the way he was while trying to control a startlingly light and bouncy ball while picking up silver jacks with the same hand. Had he any idea before this moment how clumsy he was, and how easily frustrated and distracted?

He'd won the first round, barely. Then he'd seen Rachel swing open the exit door and fly out. It took a moment for the door to close, so he could see she ran down the path unencumbered—meaning she hadn't lost one round. She didn't look back once. Evan didn't know if she was aware he was there. Her opponent lumbered up from the floor, spouting loud curses that Evan had heard and used before, but this man's word combinations were highly creative.

"This isn't fair," were his last words as he headed to the losers' bench outside.

One volunteer called, "Take it up with Justin." Three unflappable volunteers moved around the room, clarifying rules and clearing raucous disputes.

Travis won the second round, and Evan muttered, "Well done."

He shook his head. His concentration was shot, but he couldn't let that happen now. He didn't have far to go, probably just hours. If he could get it together for a few more rounds of this silly schoolyard game, he would reach the top half of the leaderboard.

With Rachel.

He had to catch up to her. At this point, he was so delirious that he didn't know if he wanted to catch up to her to beat her or to be near her.

Justin was quite possibly a diabolical psychological mastermind. How else could he have so effectively depleted Evan, physically and mentally? So far, Evan had faced his worst childhood fear, a delicious temptation, and his own flaw that would keep him from long-term happiness. When this was all over, win or lose, he'd need a long Epsom salt soak and six months of twice-a-week therapy with the best shrink he could afford so he could forget all this.

Forget *her*.

He felt his brows crush toward each other as Travis handed him the little bouncy ball. Evan drew in the steadiest breath he could and tossed the jacks up in the air.

***

Rachel knew the few men on the bench behind her gave her dirty looks as she sprinted away from them, but she let it spur her on rather than faze her. Those runners were effectively done. In fact, the only person in front of her at this point, she was almost positive, was Dora, the woman who'd braided her hair. The woman Rachel had encouraged not to give up when things got difficult and challenging. She was glad the young woman had taken the wisdom to heart and gotten further than she'd expected, but Rachel felt a little twinge of—discomfort. Could she lose to the younger woman?

No, no way. There was still time. Runners had been passing one other for days now, but anyone could be thwarted at any time. Like all the guys who were put out of the race by a few rounds of jacks.

Would Evan be one of them? Had she seen the last of him?

The discomfort came back, and she slowed down a bit

as she allowed herself to examine her emotions from every angle.

Then she realized she was slowing because her traitor of a subconscious was giving Evan an opportunity to catch up. So she could run with him again, talk to him again, be near him again.

This guy was Kryptonite to her ambition and goals. She'd refused her whole life to put a man, any man, in front of her job, her athletic goals, and anything else she set out to achieve. She'd seen women give up their dreams for men and seen them regret it. She'd also seen women give up their dreams for men and not regret it, but those women were in denial and would come to regret it someday.

She ran faster. She was so worn out, and suddenly lonely, but she also knew the mind could be a most skilled saboteur. She wouldn't let it take advantage of her fatigue. Not yet. Not until this was over.

She liked Evan. She did. Maybe even a few shades deeper than *like*. She could admit that to herself. She didn't love being alone every day, not being in a relationship, not having a partner. But at some unidentifiable moment in the last few years, she'd come to terms with the idea that it wasn't to be. By his own admission, Evan wasn't the commitment type, so it was just as well she wasn't getting attached.

She heard a snap in the brush behind her, so she turned her head and squinted over her aching shoulder. Evan?

Squirrel.

She *wasn't* getting attached. She pumped her arms to get up a small hill, and when she got to the top, she realized she was clenching her back teeth.

Burpees, jacks, pushups, buckets of sand, puzzle boxes, barbed wire, dark water, and unfamiliar woods. All of that, and the one thing that had gotten in her head, pushed its way into her psyche, was a muscled, self-deprecating, funny, generous, smart, sexy English socc—*football* star.

Nope. Just nope. No way.

This race was hers, and it was better for everyone—including dozens of kids at her school—if Evan Hughes got left on the jacks bench. He could be proud of how far he'd come for someone who'd never done anything like this before. He could be proud to lose to her, and she had a feeling he would be.

For some reason, that wreaked the most havoc on her emotions. He respected her competence and the fact that she was strong, ambitious, and driven. It wouldn't wound his male pride to lose to her.

Even if he'd worked so hard. Even if he'd fought through his fear of water. Even if he'd put her shoulder back in place. Only one of them could win, after all. And it had to be her. Her kids needed the money—and to see how hard work could pay off—more than Evan needed to win.

Why would he need this as a comeback, anyway? It was probably his self-esteem that had taken a hit, what with his retirement from soccer, its adoring fans, and his public breakup. He didn't actually need this race, even if he thought he did. It was more for his own ego. Because she knew if he showed up back in his home country with that gorgeous, disarming smile, all would be forgiven and they would put him right on TV or in coaching or whatever he wanted to do. And she would read all about it online, as someone he used to know.

Because that was all that she was now. They'd had a few moments, they had had a very steamy and unforgettable night, and now she had to leave him behind.

She could cry about it when she had the luxury of time. After she won.

She saw a volunteer about a hundred yards in the distance, so she picked up her pace. Whatever this was, she'd get through it and keep going. Though she was positioned well for winning, she couldn't relax and breathe until she was the one in front and crossing the finish. It wouldn't be long now.

She slowed to a stop in front of the young female

volunteer with red hair that was a bright contrast against the woody backdrop. She held a large box that looked familiar.

"Hi, Rachel!" the volunteer said. "It's funny, I don't know any of the other competitors' names other than you and Evan Hughes." She rummaged in the box. "Here is your prize for getting this far."

"My phone!" Rachel said when the woman handed it to her. "But why?"

"The rest of the course is unmarked. I'll help you download an app with the map for the rest of the course. It has a built-in compass. You need to find your way to the finish."

Ugh. Rachel was smart, and she was resourceful. She was good at lots of things, but for some reason, she was never very good at reading maps. If confronted with a paper map, she had to turn it in the direction she was going in. And she didn't have a keen sense of direction. Races were well marked, so she'd never had an issue before. She'd have to keep moving fast, but now there was a chance she'd run miles in the wrong direction before realizing it and have to double back, losing precious minutes.

The volunteer misinterpreted Rachel's expression. "Don't worry," she said. "You're being tracked, and we wouldn't let you get really lost. Unless you're hurt or can't go on or aren't willing to go on, you can't be eliminated now. You only have to find your way. This is totally nothing for you."

She helped Rachel find and download the app and made sure she was logged in and the map was working before she gave Rachel the go-ahead. "I can't believe all these texts," Rachel said when she had her phone back.

"Everyone has texts and voicemails by now. I think Justin counted on you getting distracted by those, so my advice is to ignore them. Then again, I'm not supposed to be giving you advice."

"You're right," Rachel said. "Thanks." She ran about five hundred yards from the checkpoint so any runner coming up behind her wouldn't see her, then stopped to swig some water and consult the terrain map. She was no mountaineer, and it was confusing until she realized it gave her a choice of two routes. One looked a lot longer and more twisty-turny, so she opted for the shorter and easier-to-follow route. The terrain lines swirled under the shorter route, so maybe it would be a little rougher going, but it looked to be about half the distance of the other route, so it was her choice. She assumed everyone would take the shorter route to start, and if they found they'd strayed, they would have the option of the longer one to get back to where they needed to be, though with lost time.

Her phone buzzed. Rachel knew for a certainty the volunteer was right; this was a distraction. Justin was likely counting on everyone's urge to answer whatever texts or calls had come in, and it could draw their full attention away from the map.

She wouldn't answer. She would only glance. Barely glance. To make sure there was no emergency. Not that she was in any position to help if there was one.

ARE YOU THERE? her brother Brian's text from yesterday blared. YOU GOT THIS, MORE MONEY FOR A CHICK! KEEP GOING, DON'T STOP! DOLLARS!

What was he blathering about?

Luckily her other brother, Kevin, was somewhat more literate. He'd sent his text about an hour after Brian's. RACH, THAT DUDE WHO RUNS THE RACE JUST ANNOUNCED AN EXTRA $1,000 IN PRIZE MONEY IF A WOMAN WINS. I DON'T KNOW IF YOU HAVE YOUR PHONE OR IF YOU KNOW THAT. BUT YOU GOTTA WIN THIS THING.

Rachel's eyes widened, and she stopped short to reread Kevin's text and make sure she saw what she thought she saw. An extra $1,000 if a woman won the race?

It was a stunt to keep the public's attention on the race until it was over, of course. And maybe to attract more women into next year's race. Or maybe Justin knew that

Evan Hughes getting beaten by a woman was a way better story than Evan Hughes crushing this competition, and maybe he could stretch The Golden Crucible's fifteen minutes of fame to sixteen minutes.

But who cared why he'd added an extra incentive for her to win? An extra $1,000 would go a long way in the new maker lab for the kids.

She tossed one last look over her shoulder, pitying herself for hoping to see Evan come over the hill behind her so at least he'd be close. At least—

She looked down and opened her last text. GO GIRL, Dad texted. His eyes weren't what they once were, so his texts were always brief. GO.

She went.

JENNIFER SAFREY

CHAPTER 15

Evan hadn't gotten docked a half hour because he'd emerged victorious and beaten the valiant Travis in their legendary jacks battle. That last ball bounce and catch had been so satisfying, so gratifying, and such a relief, though he'd never admit that to anyone who might ever ask.

But he had lost two rounds in the jacks game, which meant he had to run on with two encumbrances.

Two massive jugs of sloshing water. One in each hand. The volunteer had told him they were forty pounds each. Evan was strong, but the weight meant he couldn't move as fast as he needed to, to catch up to Rachel. Er, to win.

Oh, who was he kidding? He kept scanning the foreground for her chestnut braid.

He paused to lower the jugs to the ground, shake his arms, and circle his wrists. Then he hoisted the jugs up again to awkwardly hurry forward.

This was absurd. Why was he doing this? He was a grown man with some success and notoriety. This weekend was utter and complete bollocks.

There was a lesson in all this; there had to be.

What the bloody hell was it? That he was too old for this nonsense? That he deserved this torture for everything wrong he'd ever done? That the most amazing woman in the world was completely unavailable to you if you were one of those jerk non-commitment men?

He hobbled along in his best semblance of a run for what seemed like nine days before he saw the next checkpoint in the distance. He hoped the next challenge was for them to sever off each of his arms at the elbow because he preferred that to carrying these jugs for one more step.

No, the nice volunteer woman who knew his name said no limb amputation, but he was allowed to leave the jugs in exchange for his phone.

He'd never been so happy to hold a possession of his in his red and raw hands. His first thought was, *I hope I can get a signal.* His second thought was, *did I ever get Rachel's phone number?*

His third thought was, *Hughes, you're a right idiot and she's smart to get as far away from you as she can. So she can win. And for other reasons. Leave her alone.*

The volunteer then told him about how the trail was unmarked and he'd need to use a trail map app and she set him up, but he barely heard her. He was beginning to understand this race wasn't about winning anymore. This race wasn't about the race. This race was about getting at something deeper inside him. Something about—

He didn't quite know.

He jogged ahead, glancing at the map on the little screen and ignoring a few texts that had come in from his parents and his training buddy. He was on the brink of some kind of epiphany.

Or a total meltdown. But he would go with an epiphany for now.

The Golden Crucible HQ must have charged everyone's phones all weekend, because despite the fact that Evan himself was at about four percent, his battery was a full and happy one hundred. Although he had no clue where he was, he guessed he couldn't be too far from civilization if his phone was getting a signal. Which meant—this was coming to an end.

Again, thoughts tumbled in his mind like brightly colored shirts in a clothes dryer. He'd cross the finish line not too long from now, first or not, but it would be unfinished if he couldn't figure out what this had all been *for*.

He hated that feeling of unfinished business. He hated matches that ended in a tie. He'd rather lose and take the wisdom it offered than tie and get nothing out of it. He hated this limbo, having fled his country amid a scandal that he couldn't smile his way out of.

Rachel was unfinished business. He needed to get to her to finish whatever it was, make some kind of decision. But the decision to pursue something with her—he'd end up hurting her in the end, the way he had with Grace, wouldn't he? So the decision would have to be goodbye, and maybe an apology for feeling this way about her and making love to her when he knew he would end up being an idiot.

The strange thing was, he could actually see himself with her. He could envision making dinner together, sitting on a porch, drinking beer together, and taking a vacation together. He could see it and he wanted it, wanted her.

His brain circled back to Grace again and how he'd ruined everything. Before he knew it, he was searching for a number in his phone he'd been sure he'd never call again.

It rang quite a few times, no doubt with her shocked to see his name on her screen and considering throwing her phone off London Bridge.

"Evan."

It wasn't a question.

"Hello, Grace."

Silence.

"Hello?" he said again, because it would be like Justin to torture him into thinking he was calling someone he knew, only to have had all his contacts forwarded to someone on the other end who would now scream at him to drop and give him one hundred and fifty pushups.

But, "Yeah," Grace said. "Aren't you running around in the woods somewhere?"

"Literally, yes, I'm running now. Kind of slowly."

"Er ... why are you calling? From the woods? While running?"

"There are a few things I want to say to you," he said, wincing at how lame his words were.

"It's been two years. We haven't spoken a word to one another in two years, and by the way, that was fine with me. I would have been fine keeping that up. Now you go on one long mountain run in America and you feel like chatting?"

"I'm— How do you know where I am?" Grace wasn't the biggest sports fan, even when Evan played. She wouldn't have just come across the info.

"Sophie saw it on the telly and told me when I had dinner with her last night."

"How is Sophie?" he asked politely.

"She hates you. Look, what is it you want to say? Do I even want to hear it?"

"I don't know if you want to hear it or if you even care anymore."

"I *don't* care, but now you have me curious."

"I want to say I'm sorry, Grace. I'm sorry for hurting you."

Grace was quiet. "You said back then that you were sorry."

"It was different then. I was trying to make a clean break because it was difficult for me too. Everything I said came out harsher than I'd intended. But the truth is that you're an amazing woman."

"Obviously."

Evan smiled. "You truly are, and I felt terrible disappointing you. But I disappointed myself too, and I didn't know how to cope with that and—anyway, I apologize for all of it."

"This is the last thing I expected to hear today, or ever," Grace said. "I was quite insulted and embarrassed."

"I know."

"So I said all those things to the press. Because I was angry. And I wanted everyone to hate you as much as I did."

"Well done."

Grace made a scoffing sound.

"I mean it," he said. "Well done. Everyone did hate me. I'm sure lots of people still do. But I want to do things with my life and—I didn't feel right moving on until I gave this some better—closure, I suppose."

"Moving on?" Grace asked.

"Finishing this, restructuring my career."

"Oh, I thought you meant that woman you're running with."

"Rachel?"

"Rachel, is it? Not even a last name? Sophie said you looked awfully chummy with her on the telly."

"The press was asking her all kinds of stupid questions about her age, and they gave her this skimpy thing to wear, and—I don't know. I thought I should be in her corner."

"But you're trying to beat her."

"I'm not sure I will."

"Sophie said she's a lot older than you."

"Only by a few years. And that 'older woman' is a far superior all-around athlete than me."

"That's modest of you." Grace paused. "Was that all?"

"An extremely belated apology for the worst thing I ever did to someone? Yeah, that's all."

"Was it the worst thing you ever did to someone?" she asked. "Because I don't think it makes you a bad person to realize you don't love someone the way you used to or the way you thought you did."

Evan stopped and breathed out one long exhale. Then he crouched in the dirt and dropped his head in his hand. He had no idea what to say to that.

"I won't say this publicly," she added, "but I'm glad now that you had the sense to tell me how you felt before we had some elaborate wedding, before I had invested a lot more of my life in you. It hurt at the time, but if I'd known then that it was for the best, I wouldn't have come after you so hard. If you tell anyone I said that, though, I'll call you a liar."

"Fair enough."

"But I came out of it okay. I'm dating a man I really like and I haven't announced it yet because I like that it's just us. I will soon, though."

Evan searched his heart and found nothing but relief. "I'm so happy to hear that, Grace. Not that I'm surprised. I'm just happy."

"I'm not sure why I told you that."

"I won't tell anyone."

"I know. Even when I—even when the press said all those things about you, you never said anything about me."

"Because you did nothing wrong."

"Neither did you. Truly."

Evan felt an expansion in his chest, opening up space around his heart.

"Thanks for calling," Grace said after an awkward moment.

"No," he said. "Thank you. I didn't expect you to say— er, thank you."

Grace cleared her throat. "You'd better get back to it."

"Right. Cheers."

He was about to disconnect when he heard, "Wait, Evan!"

He brought the phone back to his ear. "Yeah?"

"What's her name again?"

"Who?"

"The woman who's running against you. The woman you said is such a world-class athlete."

"Rachel."

"Right. I'm one hundred percent rooting for her. I hope Rachel wipes the floor with your ass. Sophie said the news story made this out to be a Him vs. Her. And I'm always, always going to root for the Her."

"I—"

"I do still appreciate the call, but I'm rooting for the Her. No offense."

"None taken. Sisterhood and all that."

"That's right. Try not to get eaten by a bear."

"I can't promise that. Though I've managed to elude large animals so far."

"What I'm saying, Evan," she said, more softly, "is take care. I mean it."

Evan closed his eyes and nodded once. "You too, Grace."

He clicked off and remained in his crouch with the phone dangling from his hand. She'd said that he hadn't done anything bad to her. He hadn't done anything wrong. He'd only realized he hadn't loved her or hadn't loved her as much as he'd meant to.

For two years he'd tormented himself for that. He'd felt guilty, angry, confused. He'd never considered that was just how feelings were.

As he sat with it some more, it occurred to him—was it possible he *wasn't* Mr. Non-Commitment?

Was it possible that he only hadn't wanted to commit to that particular woman?

Was it possible that lovely, popular Grace hadn't been the woman for him? That he would be able to commit to the *right* woman?

The one he could imagine himself with?

The one who was getting further and further from him with each passing moment?

He needed to tell Rachel—what?

He lifted his face to the hot sun. He wiped his brow with the back of his hand.

He needed to tell her his lesson was her.

He needed to tell her *she* was the reason for all this.

Oh, God. He needed to tell her he loved her.

Angel trumpets of epiphany echoed in his exhausted brain.

He rose, his calves protesting, his knees cursing him. His heart was wide open, exposed, raw.

This race would kill him. He stood, swayed a bit, then tensed his jaw and steadied his body.

Hughes under pressure! Hughes makes his run! Hughes ... Hughes ...

Evan Hughes ran. Toward the most important goal in his life.

CHAPTER 16

Lost. Rachel couldn't get lost. She figured things out. She used best practices. She took the right action. She wasn't the kind of fool who got *lost*.

She'd been going along at a good pace, feeling confident, until she checked the GPS and realized she'd strayed off the path. She'd been running in the wrong direction for quite some time.

She'd tried to set herself straight, but without trail markers, it was frustrating. Every time she headed in what she thought was the right direction, the map proved her wrong. She'd been about to scream when she ran into two volunteers who'd tracked her wandering and accompanied her to the correct path.

Now she was on her way to the finish, but the way wasn't ahead.

The way was up.

Rachel was a city girl, through and through. She liked the outdoors and she liked hiking, but she'd always been given a route to follow. She didn't have any experience with topographical maps, or their representations of altitude. She'd seen the darker color of the shorter of the two trails she'd chosen and assumed the compromise for the shorter trail was some elevation.

She'd been right about that. What she hadn't been prepared for was how uphill it was.

She didn't need rock-climbing gear—not that she'd know how to use any—but she needed to move forward mostly on her hands and knees.

She was thirsty, but it wasn't urgent. Afraid of losing any more time, she ignored the sensation for now. Her hands were filthy, her short fingernails were a ragged disaster, and her legs were scraped up. She could have put on her sweatpants to cushion her legs, but the midday heat was unforgiving. Who knew when she'd reach the top of this and have to run really fast to get to the end? She didn't want to be overheated or bundled up.

She hadn't seen anyone ahead of her. She had to hope the map had been equally ineffective for those left in the race and that she hadn't lost so much time—or at least had lost less time than the last few contenders.

What she should have done when she was first given her phone was allow herself five minutes to go to YouTube and search "how to read trail maps" to make sure she wouldn't make a grievous error. Too late now.

Be informed, she'd told her students every damn year. *Get all the information you can. Make sure you're working with as much knowledge as is available before you try something new. It will save you time in the end.*

What an amazing teacher. Rachel wished she'd had one like her.

She reached up and grabbed a thick tree root to hoist herself up. Her shoulder burned and her foot slipped, dislodging a cluster of little pebbles and ricocheting them down the hill behind her.

"What the—" she heard. When she had her footing, she looked over her shoulder.

About twenty feet behind her. Evan Hughes.

"You!" he yelled up at her. "Almost breaking my nose at the barbed wire wasn't enough? You need to blind me with

… with … *forest pellets?*"

His words were one thing, but his tone was another, and the tone wasn't angry. It was amused, maybe even relieved.

Warmth filled her belly until her brain caught up and realized it was because she was *happy* to see Evan.

What on earth was wrong with her? An extra grand was on the line now, and she was neck and neck with him due to her own incompetence.

She should have left him at the water. She should have left him instead of making love to him.

Even as she had those thoughts, she knew she wouldn't have left him at either of those points, or anywhere in this race. And it had weakened her. She'd let this man—this amazing, sexy, funny, generous, talented man—distract her the entire race. And for what? Nothing. It wasn't as if they had a future. She was still throwing away her chance to win, to what? To be near him?

Her foot slipped again, and she cursed. If her mental game broke down now, her physical game would do the same.

Evan was closer now. She didn't need to turn around to know. She didn't need to hear the branches cracking and leaves rustling behind her. When he was near, every cell in her body flooded with warmth. He relaxed her. And she just couldn't now.

"I'm glad I caught up with you," Evan said, close behind her.

Rachel tried to propel herself forward faster. "I'll bet you are."

"Not for the reason you think, though."

"Really." Rachel kept moving. "So you're glad you caught up to me for my charming personality, then? Not to win?"

"Your charming personality is debatable. But no, not to win."

Was he trying some kind of mind-bending psych-out game? "I don't know what you're talking about," she finally said through gritted teeth. "I don't want to mess around with you right now."

"All I'm asking is to listen to me for two minutes. Two. Then you can keep going, and I'll sit here for an hour. As much time as it takes for me to be out of the race for good."

Rachel did stop then. She turned around and sprawled face up on the ground. "What?"

He climbed a few more feet to fall next to her. His sneaker touched hers and she shifted her foot an inch so it wasn't. "This race is yours to win," he said. "I'm exhausted. And I don't need to win anymore. I got what I wanted out of all this."

"What?" Rachel asked again, feeling like an idiot. Maybe it was the heat, the weariness, and the thirst, but she'd thought she heard him say he didn't want to win anymore because he got— "What?"

"Clarity," he said. "I entered this race because I thought I knew what I wanted and that winning would help me get it. Instead, the last two days have shown me I want something completely different."

"Are you kidding me right now?"

He smiled, and it was brighter than the sun cooking her arms and legs. "No, I'm not. I've been laboring under the idea that a win would get me back the life I used to have, or something very much like it. A place in the public eye again, maybe a commentator. I'd completely forgotten that I retired from football not only because I'm getting up there in age, but because I'm tired of it. I did everything I could do. I loved it, but it's time to look to the next phase in my life, not try to go back."

"I don't understand why—"

"Let me get this out," Evan interrupted quietly. "There's more to life than sport, right? There's more. You love racing, right? But it's not your purpose. You're a teacher. You have influence and fulfillment. You help kids every day with moving toward their dreams. That's purpose."

He paused, maybe waiting for affirmation. She gave it

with a nod.

"I've been thinking that I've done all right for myself, and it doesn't need to be about me anymore. I'm going to start a foundation. A charitable foundation, to raise money to help kids reach their dreams."

Rachel blinked. "Wow. That's—wow. That's amazing. And this came to you while you were … running?"

"It's more like he came to me and helped me."

"Who—?"

"I'll tell you that later," he said. "There's more important stuff I need to say."

Rachel looked up, then back at him. "I appreciate what you're saying means a lot to you, but do you think maybe it can wait just a little longer, until this is over?"

"No," he said. "I've been running a long time, you see. Not just this weekend. And it's been you I've been running after. I just didn't know it until now."

Rachel's head started to spin. Maybe she should drink some water after all.

"You," he said, "are the woman for me. You challenge me. You make me better. You are everything I aspire to be as a human being. My life will be brighter and bigger with you in it, and I want to give the same to you. I want to give."

Rachel couldn't speak. Her mouth couldn't make words, though she felt herself moving her lips around like a goldfish spilled out of a bowl, desperate for air.

"I'm going to lose this race," he said. "I'm tired, and I don't care because I know what I want now. That's what this stress and pain and mental suffering was all for. And maybe you'll win, and I'll be so happy. Or maybe you'll lose. I don't know what kind of loser you are. But I have a feeling that no matter how bad a loser you are, I'll love it."

Rachel stopped breathing.

"That's right," he said, moving his face to within an inch of hers and cupping her head in his hand. "I said *love*. I love how you fight and I love your brain and I love your body and I love your crap singing voice and I love your passion and I love your commitment, and I even love how you're looking at me now, like you want to punch me in the face. I even love the hell nightmare torture of this race because it brought me to clarity. It brought me to you. I love y—"

"Stop!" she said. "Why are you doing this now?"

He drew his hand back and retreated a bit. "I—I told you why."

Rachel's chest filled and collapsed with heavy, emotional breaths. "This is almost over! I'm almost there! I can get the money for—and this is why you stopped me?"

"Rachel, it doesn't matter. The money doesn't matter. Listen to what I'm saying—"

"I have been, and you're telling me you love me, and it's a *useless* thing to say because you have said you can't commit to a relationship. Now you're holding me back for what? Just to start something we can't see through?"

"No, I forgot to tell you, no—I can. I can commit. I realized I can because I—"

"Save it!" she cried. "Again, this is happening. Again, here I am with a man trying to hold me back, this time for a future that you told me doesn't exist!" She felt herself shaking. She would lose him, now or later. She couldn't lose this race too.

Then they would all have nothing. At least, if she won, the kids in her school, current and future, would have opportunities they didn't have now. Opportunities she didn't have as a kid, in a one-income family in a neighborhood with a school that had few resources.

"A man trying to hold you back?" he asked, his volume rising with each word. "Hold *you* back?"

Rachel turned around and scrambled away from him, but she couldn't get far, her feet slipping on rocks in her anger and frustration. "That's what you *all* do! That's—"

"You really think that's what it is? That men, men in general, are competitive idiots? We're all the problem?" His voice got fainter. He wasn't coming after her.

"Run!" she screamed into the dirt. "Evan, just run! Go!

Finish this!"

"No!" he roared back.

She slammed her fists into the dirt and screamed from her gut, every ounce of emotions blending into one long wordless vowel.

When it ended, he yelled, "You're a bloody math and science teacher! Aren't you capable of using the logic you teach? That guy in high school you beat for school president, your boyfriend who liked that board game, your ex-husband— Why haven't you figured out the common denominator in all those equations is *you*?"

Rachel froze. Her fingers clawed fruitlessly through the dirt.

"Can you really not see *you're* the competitive one?" he shouted. "From what you said, it sounds clear as hell to me that *you* turned all those relationships into contests, not them! It was *you* who needed to be better, be on top, be superior. And in every case, you probably already were, but you needed to prove it every time. I don't think I'm going out on a limb—a bloody literal limb out here in the damn woods in the freaking middle of *nowhere*—if I say every other relationship you've had followed that pattern. It's like you're still trying to get into Harvard over and over again, even though you've done so well for yourself. It didn't matter. You have nothing to prove to anyone. But you can't stop fighting. You can't stop competing for your share."

"Shut up," Rachel said, but her voice was weak.

"Do you really need to win right now? I told you I'd donate the money, so that's not it. I think right now you just want to beat *me*."

Evan let the last word hang there, and it was a painful word because it was a true word.

"Winning would be fun," he said, "especially now that you are having a few minutes of fame. But can't you let yourself off the hook and see there's something else in front of you now? Some*one* else? I can give you a future. Let me tell you."

Rachel couldn't look at him; she was afraid—no, ashamed to. She felt more naked now with him than she had last night. How had he picked her apart and analyzed her so expertly? And was it true that he—

A low buzzing filled her ears, and though she shook her head, it seemed to get louder and louder. No, it wasn't buzzing, it was—

"Rachel, I—"

She held up her hand to silence him as she lifted her chin, listening.

No, it wasn't buzzing.

It was cheering.

The finish was near.

And if the crowd was suddenly cheering, it could only mean that someone else was—

She pushed forward, sinking her fingers and shoving the toes of her sneakers into the dirt.

"Rachel!" Evan called.

"Run!" she said, though she knew he wouldn't. But she couldn't let him keep her back any longer. She could push forward and have a chance, or she could fall back and lose, choose a man over a win, and likely lose her heart as well.

She couldn't think about how well he knew her. How despite knowing all her crap, he was willing to say—almost say—that he loved her.

She looked up and saw it. There. The top. Level ground. She wrapped her hand around a skinny tree trunk and hoisted herself up. Her shoulder was on fire again. Her legs were noodles. Her throat was dry.

Her heart hurt. So much.

She flopped onto the flat top of the hill and crawled a few inches before dragging herself to her feet. She could see it, the finish line. There were colors and people. There was music and laughing.

She was without the luxury of an extra second. She couldn't hesitate again, but she must have because she heard Evan say softly and sadly, "Go, Rachel."

She opened her mouth but closed it again, knowing the energy it took to speak would be energy depleted for this last push. He knew what she'd say, anyway. She didn't need to say it. She didn't need to apologize for being who she was at this moment in time.

Slower than she had in the last two days, she ran toward the people, the party. She stumbled with fatigue every few steps. Her lungs strained with effort to keep up. She ran for Harvard, and her dad, who'd done his best to give her all he could. She ran for the relationships she'd sabotaged and emotionally abandoned. She ran for her students. And she ran for herself, because in the successful life she'd made, it was just her. Alone.

She hoped the cheers she heard were for her, for her imminent victory, because it was too devastating to think about who she was leaving in the dirt behind her.

***

Evan dragged himself along, keeping his eyes on a chestnut braid getting further and further from him. Though no longer at a very impressive clip. Rachel was exhausted, but he had to hand it to her, she gave it every cell of her being. When she crossed the finish, winner or not, she'd have used up every ounce of reserves in her tank.

He hoped she was about to win. He truly did. The thought of her not winning was almost too hard to bear, because then her rejection of him would be for nothing.

Perhaps it hadn't been his finest moment, though he'd intended it to be. Maybe calling her out on her competitiveness in past relationships wasn't the gentlemanly thing to do. But if he'd said nothing about it, he would have been dishonest and not himself, and she didn't deserve anything but authenticity.

Not that it mattered now. She didn't believe he could give her a future, and he couldn't blame her. He'd told her before he couldn't because he'd believed it. But after talking to Grace, he was willing to believe he was different. He had been hoping Rachel would also be open-minded, that her feelings for him ran as deep as his did for her.

His brain was enveloped in fog, and he couldn't think it through anymore. He needed to finish this and go home. And get on with at least part of the new life he envisioned for himself.

He glanced to either side of him and looked over his shoulder. No one. The finish loomed on the horizon with a big blue banner waving in the sun. He'd finish just after Rachel. The corners of his mouth lifted a bit. The press would love it.

She deserves it, he said to himself in a press conference speech rehearsal. *She had so many reasons to want this more than me. And she's a far better all-around athlete than me. She is the most beautiful creature I've ever shared air with, and now that I've met her and I know she exists in the world, I don't know what I'll do without—*

Right. Probably best to leave that last part out.

***

The moment she rounded the grassy corner and saw the finish, Rachel knew she had lost.

She knew it because the spectators and photographers who lined either side of the path leading to and beyond the banner weren't looking in her direction, waiting for her to come into view—they were looking the other way while they cheered.

Which meant someone else had arrived before her.

She forced herself to swallow back every misstep she'd made in the last two days, every mistake, every hesitation, every stupid thing she'd done to ruin her race, and pumped her arms, trying to arrive faster.

Because even if she'd lost, she would do it strong.

When she had about two hundred feet to go, people turned her way and cheered, maybe a little louder than she'd have expected for the second-placer.

"Go Rachel!"

"Almost there!"

"You got this!"

She didn't feel the tears drop from her eyes, didn't realize she was crying until the tears ran down her hot, sweaty face. She'd never cried before, win or lose. Maybe it was exhaustion. Or Evan's revelations to her—that he loved her, that he somehow decided he now could commit, that her past relationship failures were no one's fault but her own. She dragged it all forward with her, and it was far heavier than a weighted backpack or a bucket of rocks. Worse, she knew that when the race was over, she couldn't drop it and walk away in relief. She'd drag this home with her and everywhere she went for the foreseeable future.

People held out their hands for her to slap, and she glanced over her shoulder to make sure no one else was close before she allowed herself to slow a bit and indulge in their encouragement. She tried to smile, but it felt odd on her face, like she wasn't doing it right. She recognized the faces of some of the competitors who'd started out with her and were eliminated or had dropped out before the end. Funny how they all looked happier than she felt.

Hands patted her back as she ran. To the right of the finish banner, she saw Evan's crazy soccer fan, giving her a thumbs-up. On the other side of the finish, she saw Justin clapping his hands and motioning her in.

She crossed and finally stopped.

It was over.

Someone hung a medal around her neck. People were still screaming her name. Justin walked over to her with his hand out.

"Did I—" Rachel asked, confused. "Am I—?"

"I'm really proud of you, Rachel," Justin said, shaking her hand firmly and clapping her on her wrecked shoulder with his other hand. She tried not to flinch from the scalding pain. "And thanks for making this so amazing. To have you two finish on top—"

"Us two...?"

And over his shoulder, she saw Dora. Dora, with a huge smile on her face. Dora, with a garland crown on her head.

Dora, the winner.

"Two women," Justin said, "coming in one-two."

Dora shoved Justin aside. He laughed as she grabbed Rachel and hugged her. "Rachel! We did it! You did it! You inspired me. Thank you. Thank you."

"Nothing makes me happier and more satisfied," Justin said, "than to watch two ladies crush these macho guys. It's a great thing for The Golden Crucible."

Dora hadn't let go. Rachel wrapped one arm around the joyful younger woman.

"Oh, my God," Dora said into her ear. "This was so hard. I wanted to give up so many times. But when I was braiding your hair, you told me not to. Do you remember? And I kept thinking about how the press treated you and I knew that we girls had to stick together, that I had to push too, even when I wanted to stop, and oh, my God, I wanted to stop so many times. But now, this is the best thing I ever did. I feel like I can do anything after today. Thank you. Thank you."

Rachel closed her eyes and made a sound that wasn't quite a laugh or a sob. Dora's T-shirt was damp, and Rachel rested her head on her shoulder.

Dora lifted her head, looked behind Rachel, then spun Rachel around. "Look! Here he comes!"

Cameras flashed. People screamed again. "Hughes! Evan Hughes!"

Watching him jog toward the finish filled Rachel's heart with a flash of light, even though she knew she had to start *not* feeling that way. She knew his body now, knew how he moved, and she could tell by his short strides and his tense jaw that he was in pain. He wasn't battling it, though; he was moving through it enough to get the job done. He smiled at the people who reached out to high-five him, back-pat him, and touch this celebrity athlete. And it was only now that Rachel was able to realize that many of the spectators were in soccer shirts, some with HUGHES on the back. Evan was unsurprised that people had come out to see him. He'd had years to get used to the attention. Before he crossed the finish, he veered to the corner and gave his super-fan a heartfelt hug.

His kindness wasn't lost on everyone, who cheered even louder.

No one was behind him, so he casually walked across the finish.

Then he was right in front of her. His eyes lit into hers for the barest moment before his face broke into a big grin. He held out his arms for both women to hug him.

"I've never been so happy to lose," he said. All three of them rocked a bit, mostly out of fatigue. "You two were brilliant. Really."

"Great job," Rachel muttered. She was trying to memorize the smell of him.

"Oh, my God," Dora said, "Evan Hughes is hugging me. Hopefully this will be online everywhere so my friends will be jealous."

All three of them laughed. "That's not what they'll be jealous of," Evan said.

Rachel felt his back vibrate under her hand as he spoke. "They'll be jealous of what a badass you are."

"No," Dora said. "My friends will not care about that at all. They'll want to know what cologne you wear."

"It's designer," Evan said. "Eau de Third Place."

They laughed and drew apart. Rachel didn't imagine Evan's slightest flinch away from her. It hurt.

Dora couldn't be sweeter. Rachel had lost because of her own shortcomings, and she couldn't be disappointed that this young, determined woman had been, well, had been like Rachel herself. When Rachel wasn't in the middle of falling in love.

Love?

Yeah, love. The word Evan had actually said to her. The word she'd literally screamed at him for and fled from.

Justin stepped back over to the trio. "There are about half a dozen guys left to finish," he said. "But they've got a way to go. You can go get hydrated and get some food while we see all the other finishers in. Then the three of you can say a few things to the reporters, all right?"

Rachel opened her mouth to speak, but Evan beat her to it. "Rachel needs medical attention," he said. "She dislocated her shoulder yesterday."

Justin put a hand on Rachel's back and gently led her away from Evan and Dora, toward a medical tent. She was grateful for something else to occupy her mind. Between eighty-five hundred dollars and Evan's smile, she didn't want to think any more about the things she'd lost, things she'd never really had.

"Don't tell Dora," Justin said as they walked, "and don't tell Hughes either, but I had my bets down on you, kid."

Rachel kept her eyes on the tent. "You know that doesn't make me feel better about losing, right?"

"Eh, it's just money."

Rachel blinked. "You said at the start of the race that you wanted to keep the money for yourself."

"Of course, I did," he said. "But that's just blather I say to motivate these chumps. Look, you and that other girl coming in the two top spots shows it's not a fluke for a woman to win. I tried to make this a tough few days for all of you, and you two were physically and mentally the toughest. That will encourage a lot of little girls out in the world."

Rachel stopped and looked at him. "That's an admirable thing to say."

"I have a wife," Justin said. "I have four sisters. I have two daughters. I have a woman working for me who manages The Golden Crucible HQ. I'm surrounded by women, and I can't outsmart any of them, ever. I've designed several of The Golden Crucible races now, and I'm finally satisfied with my work because if you two came out on top, I know I designed it so that truly the best athletes win."

"I appreciate that."

"So do I, kid."

"You know you're like ten years younger than me, right?"

"Age is just a unit of measurement, a number. The way you fight, the way you compete—anyone can see you're just a pushy, determined kid."

Rachel smiled, then frowned. "The way I compete? You—saw me?"

"I couldn't let anyone get hurt. I had eyes on everyone as often as I could."

They were quiet a moment, then Rachel said, "Then you saw—"

"Some fascinating things. I saw people helping each other. I saw people getting mad at each other. I saw people facing their fears. I saw people making decisions. I didn't see anything private in tents, and I couldn't hear anything at all, but I was aware of pretty much everything that happened out in the open on the course. But also—I didn't watch it. You understand?"

She nodded. "Thanks."

They approached the medical tent. "Take care of yourself, kid. I'll see you in a bit, and I'll have a beer waiting for you. I'm also going to have a line of people who want autographs and a meet-and-greet if you're up to it."

She took a steadying breath. She'd been famous for a couple of days—if reluctantly—and that fame came with obligations. "For you, sure. And make that beer a cold water, or three."

Justin went to pat her on the shoulder, thought better of it, and withdrew his hand. He smiled a warmer smile than Rachel had thought three days ago he was capable of, then headed back toward the festivities.

Rachel moved into the shade of the medical tent.

***

After the press conference was over, after he had publicly lauded and congratulated the two women who'd bested him, after he had signed autographs and met lots of happy fans, Evan flopped facedown onto the scratchy hotel bedspread and proceeded to not move a muscle for quite some time.

He had reserved his hotel room for one last night, having correctly predicted he wouldn't feel like traveling right after he finished. Still, he hadn't expected every single bone in his body to hurt, and he definitely hadn't expected his heart to feel sick.

The aching bones was overexertion—and age. He'd retired because he wasn't being put into matches that last season. Instead, he was watching a younger man play his position much of the time. And he was angry because he'd worked so hard for years and he didn't deserve to get shut out.

But with the benefit of time away, and the experience of this weekend, he far better understood the reasons he wasn't played. He was slower. He ran slower, he reacted slower, and he hurt more, and that was a fact of aging. He was still a great athlete, but he wasn't quite what he used to be. And it was okay, because he was ready to be something different and be the best at that.

The sick heart was because he wouldn't get to be the best with the best woman he'd ever met.

It was strange, Evan thought, how you lived your whole life easily without meeting someone—then you met them, and suddenly you felt you would never be able to make it without them. You completely forgot you breathed and ate and walked before with no issue. You forgot you had been just fine.

But Evan Hughes had never been happy with just fine. Evan far preferred epic. Now that he'd met a woman who lived every moment for epic, he'd never be the same.

He rolled over and picked up the receiver from the phone on the nightstand. He paused a brief moment, marveling at the foreign feel of an actual land telephone in his hand, then pressed zero.

"Yes," he said when the receptionist picked up. "Could you please connect me to the room of another guest at this hotel, Rachel Bowen?"

What he would say to Rachel, he had no idea. But now that the race was no longer at stake, now that the pressure was off, maybe she could hear him. Maybe she could see what he saw. Maybe he wouldn't have to say anything and she'd walk into his arms.

He heard the receptionist tap a few keys. "I'm sorry, Mr. Hughes," he said, "but Ms. Bowen has checked out."

"Checked out? When?"

"Well, she only just—though I'm not allowed to—"

"Thank you." Evan dropped the phone and was out the door before he could take another breath.

CHAPTER 17

The obstacles Evan had faced in the last forty-eight hours seemed like a civilized tea time when compared to running down the carpeted hallway on overworked legs; flying down the echoey stairwell, pulling himself along the handrails with exhausted arms; chasing a finish he wasn't even sure was there.

He crashed through the stairwell door a bit too dramatically into the blue-and-beige lobby. A woman on the sofa looked up from her complimentary newspaper and a man at the front desk scowled at him for a moment before rearranging his expression to more neutral, perhaps having recognized their famous guest.

Evan scanned the lobby and every person in it. Then he rushed to the automatic revolving door and was forced to wait two beats while it slowly turned. He huffed hard through his nose as he looked through the glass door, searching. When he could step into the revolving door, he did, moving slowly, slowly until it deposited him on the other side. He looked left and saw no one.

He looked right and saw hair. Chestnut hair.

She was bent over a rolling suitcase, adjusting a zipper. When she straightened, she saw him.

He walked up to her, his heart pounding. Rachel's hair, released from its braid and washed, was a shining tumble, catching the sun in individual strands. She wore a simple black T-shirt and jeans with one ripped knee, and combat-style boots with thick rubber soles. A silver chain dropped a black faceted stone into the hollow of her collarbone. Her left arm was cradled in a black sling.

A crease showed between her eyebrows and a frown lingered on her lips as she waited for him to speak. He wished he'd at least planned an opening sentence.

"Hi," he said. For crying out loud.

She nodded once.

"Where are you going?" he continued, just as stupidly.

"Home," she said, looking surprised, likely because he'd asked her to articulate the obvious.

"That's it?" he asked. "You're just leaving without—that's it?"

"The race is over," she said. "I lost. You lost. We're both responsible for that outcome."

"Are we?"

"How are you asking me that? You know we distracted each other—"

"Yes," he said, "we did, and I'm not the least sorry for that. Even if we hadn't, Dora still had experience with terrain maps."

At the press conference, Dora had mentioned she grew up nearby and was familiar with the land as a hiker. She had been reading terrain maps for years.

"That didn't have to matter if we'd been far enough ahead—"

"But it may have mattered that she's a good twenty years younger than us."

Rachel looked as though she'd been struck in the face. "I can't believe you—"

"Said that? Come on. You're a superior athlete, all around the best this weekend, but if you had been in the shape you're in now two decades ago, you would have finished far ahead of everyone else."

Her face hardened and she opened her mouth, but he beat her to it. "I'm sorry, but it's just a fact. Getting older slows us down, little by little. It's why I retired. Do you think I wanted to give up the thing I was good at, the thing that paid me so well and made me famous? I didn't. But my body had limits, and I hit those limits. It's what happens. And, frankly, there was no way for us to predict how strong Dora was. Not only was she a better athlete than any of us knew, her age gave her an edge."

"But if we—"

"Why do you need this to be our fault?" he asked. "What would you tell your students if they got an A- instead of an A? You'd say, if you tried your best, you can be proud."

"But I didn't try my best."

"Didn't you? Didn't you make me push your shoulder into place? Didn't you take a hard paintball hit to the chest? Didn't you beat *my* sorry ass in the end?"

"I told you to keep going! You stopped trying!"

"Because I was exhausted! Because I didn't have it in me to physically take any more. I saw you barrel toward the finish with the 'Chariots of Fire' theme going, and I could barely take another step. I didn't *let* you win. I was done. This wasn't the World Cup. If I'd gone any longer, I would have gotten injured. And you know what? I don't care that I couldn't push any harder. I lost nothing and gained everything. Because this race made me realize what I want to do with my life. And it brought me to you. My priorities shifted, and I was hoping—"

"You were hoping mine did too?"

"Didn't they? Didn't you pull my sniveling, pathetic rear end across the pitch-black water? You could have left me there—"

"I *know*," she said. "I know that." Her good shoulder slumped a bit.

Evan couldn't bear to see his—his?—beautiful, determined warrior looking so defeated. "Well done at the press conference," he said. "You were quite gracious and genuine, and smiling for the reporters and other runners."

"Dora deserved it," she said. "And they were all celebrating me as part of it, as part of the one-two women's win. The other runners deserved graciousness too. Most of them didn't even finish. How would they feel if the silver medalist acted pissy and disappointed? How could I be a jerk about losing in front of them?"

"But it's okay to be a jerk about losing in front of me?"

"Yes," Rachel said on a huff.

Evan chuckled and Rachel pounced. "Why are you laughing at me?" she demanded.

"Because I can't believe I'm standing here trying to convince you that you did great. And that we're perfect for one another, Superstar. You know we are."

"No," she said. "If I feel like I'm being held back—"

"I don't want to hold you back. It's just changing course."

"What happens when it's more important than a race?" she asked. "What happens when—"

"When it's a relationship?" he finished gently. "We'll work together."

"We won't."

"I will."

"I won't."

Evan was too shocked to answer right away. He blinked. Her hard expression didn't change. "You ... won't?" he finally managed.

"You said it yourself," she said. "I blew it in my other relationships. You were right. Maybe I knew it all along and could never admit it to myself, or maybe I was just too stupid to see, but the ends of all those relationships were my fault. I was too competitive. I messed everything up."

"That doesn't mean you'll mess up with me."

Rachel rolled her eyes and blew out a breath through her mouth. Then she looked him in the eye. "The best predictor of future behavior is past behavior. You've heard of that,

I'm sure."

"It might be the best predictor," Evan countered, "but can you say for sure it's the only predictor?"

"No, of course not," she said, "but it's certainly the most likely."

"Was it the most likely that some kid out of nowhere clobbered both of us in The Golden Crucible? Was it the most likely that we fell in—"

Her eyes widened.

He stammered. "In—into this situation?"

"I'm forty-five," she said, "and I don't have the luxury of making stupid mistakes anymore. And you have things you want to do."

"I—"

"Go. Go do them. You shouldn't be held back either."

In the very first season of his football career, an opposing player had smashed into Evan head-on, and both of them had hit the ground. Evan had lay on the turf, gasping for air, not even remembering where he was, just staring at the deep blue sky and wondering if he'd died. He'd never been that shocked and breathless since.

Not until now.

"I'm—" Rachel began, and Evan held up a hand to cut her off. He didn't know if she was about to say *I'm sorry* or *I'm late* or *I'm never speaking to you again*, but he didn't want to hear whatever it was.

They stood in charged silence for a moment.

He suddenly recalled the guy he saw eliminated the first night at the monkey bars, who yelled at the volunteer in anger and protest, but that anger wouldn't change the fact that he was out.

Sometimes you were simply defeated. Evan knew that. Sometimes you did all you were capable of, but you were defeated and you couldn't change it, and it was better to take the loss and go home. Maybe learn something from it later, if you were lucky.

This would be the last time he'd be this close to Rachel

Bowen. He didn't want that to be true, but he couldn't change it.

"You said you'd beat me," Evan said. "You did. Well done."

He turned and walked alone toward the rest of his life.

CHAPTER 18

"Ms. Bowen! Ms. Bowen!"

Rachel turned, wincing a bit as the strap of her book bag slid onto the sore spot on her shoulder. She smiled at the two junior-year girls laughing and hurrying to her. Both brown-skinned with beautiful smiles. Aisha was taller, gangly, with feet that turned just a bit awkwardly in. Maya was more poised and graceful. But both girls had enough brilliant, crackling currents in their brains to power every streetlight in Boston. They each clutched a cell phone covered with glittery stickers in one hand and balanced books in the other. They screeched to a stop in front of Rachel, their shoes squeaking on the floor.

"What's up?" Rachel said, genuinely happy to talk to them.

The two girls started talking over one another so quickly, Rachel closed her eyes and shook her head. "Whoa, whoa, whoa," she said, laughing. "One at a time! I'm an old lady. I can't process that fast."

"Come on, Ms. Bowen," Aisha said. "What are you, like, thirty?"

"Close enough," Rachel said.

"Okay," Aisha said. "So, remember Evan Hughes?"

Rachel blinked. For six weeks, she hadn't heard his name out loud. She hadn't said his name out loud. The most she'd done was type his name—once. Into Google. Two weeks ago. Because she couldn't help herself. And she discovered that he'd started the Evan Hughes Superstar Foundation to help high school students achieve their dreams. She couldn't read past the first two paragraphs before shutting her laptop and feeling—things she'd never felt.

Superstar...

She'd been having a harder and harder time remembering why she'd said no to him.

"Evan *Hughes*?" Aisha repeated, and Rachel realized she'd paused too long.

"The guy from your *race*?" Maya said.

"She knows that," Aisha said. "She whooped his ass."

"Hey," Rachel said automatically.

"Sorry, Ms. Bowen."

"Tell her! Tell her what we did," Maya said to Aisha.

"Okay," Aisha said, taking a dramatic breath. "So I read that Evan Hughes started this new organization to donate money to high schools and stuff, and I know you're like his friend and everything—"

"What?" Rachel asked.

"We saw you guys on TV," Maya said. "It was totally obvious you were—" Aisha signaled with her eyebrows to her classmate.

"Friends," Maya finished. She hit Aisha's arm. "So what if I say they looked like they liked each other? You saw it. Everyone saw it."

Rachel tried hard not to wince. "You were saying...?" she prompted.

"We called his foundation," Aisha said. "Me and Maya. And we told the woman on the phone that we were your students and that we need some money for our maker lab."

"Because that lab is *sitting* there," Maya said. "And I want to *make* things."

Many kids did. It drove Rachel crazy every day to walk

by the two big rooms of lab tables they'd dedicated to the tech learning they now couldn't afford to have there. But—

"So she said Maya and I could fill out this long crazy application with a bunch of essays and other stuff about what we need and what we can use it for and how it will help the students succeed, and we did our best to answer for everyone," Aisha continued.

"We scanned the application back to her from Emma's house," Maya cut in. "And today, we got it!"

Rachel blinked. "What do you mean, got it?"

"We got money!" Aisha said, and paused for a quick victory dance with Maya. "The foundation sent the school a check *and* a big box with a 3D printer to put in the lab immediately, and they said in the office that they were going to talk to you about figuring out what else to spend the money on!"

Rachel leaned against a locker and let her bag slide off her shoulder. "How do you know that?"

"Our names were on the application so they called us down to tell us the school got the money—I don't know how much, but they were excited about it—and the printer. They said they're going to announce it to the whole school on Friday but they wanted to tell us first."

"You guys," Rachel hugged each of them hard. "What an amazing thing you did. A generous thing for your classmates, and you created a legacy for students who will come after you and be able to build on what *you* helped create. You. You took initiative. It's very hard to get a grant like this, you know. You must have made quite a case for our school, and all of us."

"It took us about a week to make that application the best it could be," Aisha said. "It was actually pretty hard, but you inspired us."

"Me?"

"Yeah, you, Ms. Bowen!" Maya said, pointing at her. "Because you got out there and you got dirty and ran your ass off—sorry—for us. It was a hard race. We read after it was over what you all had to do. Swimming and carrying heavy stuff and running, like, an insane number of miles. I mean, I can't even."

"And you did all that for us," Aisha added.

"I never said that to you guys," Rachel said. "What makes you think that I—"

"Because I remember a few months ago, you lost a race, and we all knew you were trying to win prize money then. So we were pretty sure you were trying again for us. Unless you weren't. Maybe you were trying to make a down payment on a house."

"Or buy a motorcycle," Maya said.

Rachel smiled. "No, you're right. I was trying again for you. And I felt terrible that I couldn't get it for you."

"Why do you put that weight on yourself?" Maya asked. "Why do you carry around that kind of responsibility for us? You're not a millionaire, I don't think. You're not our parents. Why would you bust your—uh, butt, and *twice*, to get us money?"

"Because I—" Rachel started, and stopped. She didn't want to say to them that life was hard, because they knew, and that it was even harder for kids raised with disadvantages, because they knew that too, and that she'd gone into The Golden Crucible thinking she was their only—

"You give us a lot of hope, Ms. Bowen," Aisha said. "You know? But you're not our only hope."

In the New Hampshire woods, after carrying the extra pounds in her backpack a long way, Rachel's legs had been shaking and she'd been cursing and hurting, and then she'd finally been relieved of the burden. She'd still been tired, and she'd had a long way left to go.

But she was suddenly lighter.

So much lighter.

Maybe ... maybe she could ...

"Anyway," Maya cut into her thoughts, "the money is a surprise and we were told not to tell anyone, but we wanted

216

to tell you before everyone else so you had time to get ready."

"Get ready for what?" Rachel asked.

The girls looked at each other. "Evan Hughes is coming here," Maya said.

Rachel felt a rush in her ears. She was aware of having to keep a composed face in front of her students, but she couldn't tell if she was succeeding. "Um ... what?"

"He's coming here Friday for the announcement, and to give the award in person and talk to the student body and take pictures and whatever," Aisha said. "He's going to be giving all the recipient schools their awards in person. This is actually the first school the foundation is giving money to."

"But," Rachel said, trying very hard to process the information quickly enough, "you said get ready?"

"Because he's *coming here*," Maya said, "and you guys are ... friends."

"And now you know it's Friday," Aisha said, "so you can ... look extra nice that day."

"You always look nice, though," Maya said quickly.

"You know what I mean," Aisha said and peered into Rachel's face. "Maybe you can put on some eyeliner?"

"Listen," Rachel said, "though I always appreciate a good makeup tutorial, Hughes has seen me covered in mud and sweat, lying on the ground with a dislocated shoulder, and with sticks and twigs in my hair. I'm pretty sure that just taking a shower that morning will be an improvement on what he's seen. Not that I care," she added.

The girls smiled at her, a little bit too knowingly.

"Would you girls mind if I let the office know that I know about all this?" Rachel asked. "You said they're planning to talk to me anyway. I may be able to come in after hours the next couple of nights and set up the 3D printer so it's all ready to use Friday when the announcement is made and—" *and Evan is here.*

Something weird was happening in her chest.

"Awesome!" Aisha yelped.

"Don't tell anyone else, though," Maya said.

"I promise I won't," Rachel hurriedly said. The bell rang, startling all three as they happened to be standing right under it. Aisha and Maya said a fast goodbye and ran, giggling, hair flying, and breaking off into two different directions at the end of the hallway. Doors slammed one after the other, the breezes kicking a stray piece of notebook paper into the air and carrying it away from Rachel.

The hall had that electric hum that always remained for a few moments after all the students disappeared into their respective classrooms, the frenetic teenage energy needing time to dissipate.

Rachel walked slowly down the hallway to the main office.

Some mornings she arrived at the school, flipped on the lights in her classroom, and thought to herself, *I'm still in high school*. But it didn't depress her—quite the opposite. She'd always loved school and learning, and somehow had always known teaching was her destiny.

It had taken her a while to accept that Harvard hadn't been her destiny.

And she was still wondering if Evan—

She picked up her pace, a plan forming in her mind.

***

Evan offered an arm to each of the young women—Maya and Aisha—who were the honored ambassadors of the event and tasked with walking him to the new lab and showing him around before the schoolwide assembly, where the surprise announcement would be made and he would give an inspirational talk about following your aspirations and never giving up.

It would be nothing they hadn't heard before from Rachel Bowen, he was sure.

The hallways were quiet between classes. Evan had

never had a reason to step into an American high school before, but it felt familiar, thanks to the movies and TV shows.

"Are you both seniors?" Evan asked.

"Juniors," Maya answered.

"Not too soon to be thinking about college majors," he said. "Any ideas?"

"Transportation engineering," Aisha said.

"Roads and bridges and such?"

"Yup," she said with a grin. "I'm going to cure rush hour."

"I hope so. And you'll be the most famous woman on the planet when you do," he said. "What about you?" he asked Maya.

"Astrophysics," she responded, more shyly than her friend. "How, um, the universe is evolving, and what the end of it will be like."

"You two are quite impressive," he said. "When I was your age, my main concern was trying to look cool when heading a ball."

"They probably didn't know about CTE back then," Maya said.

Evan tried not to smile. Leave it to two brilliant girls like these to be zero impressed by a professional footballer. An old one, at that.

They walked him through one room, talking excitedly about the plans for the equipment and the afterschool clubs the math and science department had been planning. They moved through an open doorway to an adjoining room, and there was Rachel, seated at a lab table in the middle of the room.

The most complicated woman he'd ever met was wearing a simple blue top, a simple gold chain, and a simple low ponytail. She was the brightest thing in the evolving universe. Her smile was genuine, but nervous.

"Ms. Bowen!" Aisha said. "We thought you were in the auditorium. The principal told us to show Mr. Hughes around."

"Hi, Ms. Bowen," Evan said.

"Hello, Mr. Hughes," she said, and her voice around his name weakened him to his core.

No one said anything for a few moments.

"Ummm," Aisha said quickly, "so this is the other lab, where we will put a lot of cool stuff. Okay, we have to go."

"Yup," Maya said. "We definitely have to go."

"And you can catch up," Aisha finished. "Okay, bye!"

The two girls hurried out and slammed the door intentionally hard.

"You look ... good," Evan said lamely.

"So do you," she said. "You don't even look jet lagged."

"Jet lagged?" He was taken aback a moment. "Oh, I didn't come here from London. I haven't been back there. I've been staying with my buddy in Rhode Island while I look for a house."

"A house ... here?"

"Yes," he said. "England to *New* England feels right. Starting fresh."

"Right," she said. She pushed her chair back and stood. "It will be a nice program this afternoon," she said. "I'll say a few words about how we're going to develop the lab..."

"I hope the grant is enough to do everything those future engineers and astrophysicists need."

"It's more than twice The Golden Crucible prize money. It's more than enough. For a great start."

"Just so you know," he said, "this was the first school I was planning on giving the money to anyway. I got quite a bit of publicity after the event and was able to fundraise quickly. But I'll let those two students of yours believe that it was their application that did it. It would have if I hadn't already planned on this grant. They're amazing."

"They are."

"I can see your influence."

"Listen," Rachel said, "they're going to give you a nice plaque and flowers. But I have one more award for you."

She came around the front of the lab table and held out her hand. In it was a medal.

It wasn't silver or bronze; it was a golden hard plastic. But it had a laurel border and a very clear acronym.

"Most Valuable Player?" Evan asked, searching her eyes.

"Most Valuable *Person*," she said. She lifted it by its red, white, and blue striped ribbon and extended her arms to him. He bowed forward and let her drop it around his neck.

"I made it," she said, gesturing to machinery in the corner of the room, "with our school's new 3D printer. I came in the last few nights to set up the printer, and let me tell you, I made a couple of very crappy medals before I got it right."

Evan Hughes had held dozens of trophies aloft in his many years. They had all made him proud, but none of them had burst his heart open like this medal.

"You, Evan Hughes," she said, "are my most valuable person. You had faith in me—us. You believed in us. You made me better because—"

Tears shone in her eyes, and Evan resisted the overwhelming urge to take her in his arms.

"You made me better because you not only thought I was a superhero, but you showed me my Kryptonite. You saw how I've been screwing up, and you told me."

"I was angry—" he started, but she held up her hand.

"You were right," she said. "Maybe I knew all along my competitiveness was pushing men I cared about away, and I didn't want to admit it because I thought it would mean I had to limit my potential. But now that I see the way I am, I can change."

"Wait. What?"

"I can change. I can be more of a partner. I can be satisfied being an equal. I can—"

"No," he said. "No."

Rachel's face fell. "No?"

"I don't want you to change," he said. "I love the competitiveness. I never meant to make you believe you have to change. I don't *want* you to be different."

"But I—"

He put his hands on either side of her head and pressed his forehead to hers so there were only centimeters between their gazes. "Yes, you're the one who created the contests in your other relationships. But unlike those men, it doesn't threaten me. I'm up for it. I'm *up* for it, Superstar."

He opened his arms and backed up two steps. "Challenge me, fight me, push me. Throw down the gauntlet every damn day if you want. I'll love besting you once in a while. And I'll love losing to you all the other times. Because you'll love it and I want to see you happy."

A tear escaped her eye and her bottom lip wobbled.

"You're the woman who helped me realize what my next chapter in life would be. Why wouldn't I want you making *me* better for the rest of my life?"

She brushed the back of her hand across her eyes. "The rest of your life, huh? Mr. No-Commitment?"

"All I needed was to find the right Ms. Commitment."

"You were trying to tell me," she said. "I'm sorry."

"The finish line was in sight," he said. "Never a good time for a deep conversation."

She stepped forward and kissed him. And kissed him and kissed him and kissed him. He never wanted it to end.

But it had to because they had students to make happy. When they broke away, she said, "You know, there are plenty of houses for sale in the Boston area."

"That's probably true," he said. "I'll need to look into that." He kissed her on the cheek, lingering an extra moment. "We'll need to look into that."

They left the lab and turned into the crowded corridor. One by one, students realized a famous athlete was walking down their hallway with their favorite teacher on his arm.

"Oh," Rachel said, "I left your plaque in my car. I have to grab it before the assembly."

"Okay," he said, releasing her arm.

She stopped midstride, looked down at her pink flats,

then looked up at him again, a smirk curling up one corner of her mouth.

"What?" he asked, looking at his own shiny dress shoes.

"I'll race you to the parking lot."

They paused, narrowed their eyes at one another, and exploded toward the double doors.

The students cleared a path, hooting and hollering. "Go, Ms. Bowen!"

"Hey! No running in the hallway!" shouted a man in a dark suit.

"Sorry, Principal Marks!" Rachel called over her shoulder. The students roared with laughter.

And Rachel and Evan crashed through the doors together into the sunshine.

THE END

JENNIFER SAFREY

ACKNOWLEDGEMENTS

It's hard to know where to start!

This is my first published book after a nearly ten-year break from writing, during which time I owned and operated a yoga studio. I'd thought I was done with writing.

But writing wasn't done with me—and I've written two full manuscripts since this one and I'm starting a third, so I don't think it ever will be.

So, thank *you*, reader, for letting me tell you this story. I promise there will be many more.

Thank you, Melissa Keir, for giving this book a home at Inkspell Publishing. I'm very grateful and proud.

Thank you, Audrey Bobak, for your superb editing skills—your word finesse and your blooper-catching is much appreciated.

I've only competed in a few short obstacle-course races as a very amateur weekend warrior, so for this book I recruited some beta readers who have much more experience than me, and they were phenomenally helpful with details! Thank you to Cassie Caldwell, Samantha Hansen, Darcy Barnes, Deidra Shubert, and Laura E. Kammerer for so much valuable insight.

Thank you to my longtime critique partner, author Bobbi Lerman, for all your help in getting this into shape. (And for my so-far favorite review of this book: "You know I don't give a f*ck about sports, but I *love* this book!")

Thank you to The Art Friends for their daily support and camaraderie, talented women who love writing as much as I do: Shelagh Braley Starr, Dottie Grant Cohen, Michelle Bermas, and Bobbi Lerman.

Thank you to my two feline coworkers, Kimura and

Potus. True, you aren't much help with plotting, but you make every writing session very cozy.

And Theodore Kechris: Teddy, a million thank-yous aren't enough. You made me see that my writing career wasn't finished. You do everything to make me and the cats happy every day. You are the best life partner I could have asked for. You're stuck with me forever.

ABOUT THE AUTHOR

Jennifer Safrey is a multi-published, award-winning romance author. A native New Yorker, she lives in the Boston area with her writer boyfriend, Teddy, and their two beautiful and (mostly) well-behaved cats.

www.jennifersafrey.com
FB: www.facebook.com/jennifersafreyauthor
IG: @jennifersafrey_author
TikTok: jennifersafreyauthor

Made in the USA
Middletown, DE
22 November 2023

43293756R00137